goose chase

PATRICE KINDL

FROM THE LIBRARY OF
HEIDI
READ IT. LO... ...N IT.

D0711437

SCHOLASTIC INC.

New York Toronto London Auckland Sydney
Mexico City New Delhi Hong Kong Buenos Aires

No part of this publication may be reproduced in whole or in part, or stored in a
retrieval system, or transmitted in any form or by any means, electronic, mechanical,
photocopying, recording, or otherwise, without written permission of the publisher.
For information regarding permission, write to Puffin Books,
a member of Penguin Putnam Inc., 375 Hudson Street, New York, NY 10014.

ISBN 0-439-52039-8

Copyright © 2001 by Patrice Kindl. All rights reserved.
Published by Scholastic Inc., 557 Broadway, New York, NY 10012,
by arrangement with Puffin Books, a member of Penguin Putnam Inc.
SCHOLASTIC and associated logos are trademarks
and/or registered trademarks of
Scholastic Inc.

12 11 10 9 8 7 6 5 4 3 2 1   2 3 4 5 6 7/0

Printed in the U.S.A.   01

First Scholastic printing, December 2002

Escape

The air around me was filled with great white wings like sails, churning up winds that lifted the skirts of my gown and almost blew away my gold and ruby crown.

"You're here! You're all here!"

Eleven white Geese circled the tower.

"Ernestina, Lydia-the-Loud, Penelope!" Each goose landed as I called her name and began to preen herself irritably with her tail. "Selena, Simple Sophia, Beatrice-the-Brave, and Dorothea!" Overcome with excitement, I shouted out the last four, "Eugenia, Cassandra Big Foot, Ursula, and my own Little Echo!"

All twelve Geese (including Alberta) swiveled their long necks to stare at me. They hissed in unison as though trying to shush me and fixed me with twenty-four accusing little black eyes.

❧❧❧

"Kindl (*Owl in Love*) once again takes flight, this time proffering an engaging gaggle of a dozen geese and the orphaned Goose Girl who tends them. . . . Those familiar with the Brothers Grimm's 'The Six Swans' may not be surprised by the ending, but it's how Kindl gets there, tying up all loose ends along the way, that will hold readers' attention."
—*Publishers Weekly*

"The appropriately archaic manner in which Alexandria narrates her escape from confinement and subsequent adventures never feels clumsy or forced. . . . Readers can't help but become invested in Alexandria's sometimes comical, sometimes harrowing plight." —*The Horn Book*

TO ALEX ROEDIGER
I HOPE YOU LIKE YOUR NAMESAKE

AND THANKS TO
KIT

Contents

CHAPTER ONE

The Tower

A HARD BEGINNING
MAKETH A GOOD ENDING.
— JOHN HEYWOOD, PROVERBS

The King killed my canary today.

Now, I know full well that the customary way to begin such a tale as mine is: "Once upon a time, when wishes still came true, there lived a poor orphan Goose Girl," or some such fiddle-faddle. But what do I care for custom? 'Tis my own story I am telling and I will tell it as I please. And as I find myself plunged into it right up to the neck, I see no reason why you should not be also.

I resume.

The King killed my canary today.

He slew him with his great big hunting bow. The arrow was buried several handbreadths deep into a tree trunk and all that was left of poor Chipper was a few fluffy yellow feathers sticking out around the shaft.

"Why did you do that?" I cried, leaning down from the tower window.

The King strolled over to view his handiwork.

"That was my canary!"

"A thousand pardons, my lady," he said, bowing. The scar running down his left cheek gave him a sinister one-sided smile. "Methought 'twas a plump pigeon I might offer for your supper." He bared his teeth at me.

I stared down at him coldly. I ought never to have allowed the unfortunate bird out of his cage while the King was here. The King was bored with all this waiting about, that is why he did it. That, and because Chipper was a gift from the Prince, his rival. But in truth, the real reason he did it is because the King has got a heart like a lump of coal: black and stony. 'Tis not for nothing he is known as King Claudio the Cruel.

Much as I longed to wipe that smirk off of his face with a few well-chosen words, I kept my tongue behind my teeth until I had mastered my wrath. The King frightens me witless, even though he is out there and I am in here, with a grille of iron bars and several hundred tons of stonework between us. Though being locked up in this tower was certainly none of my choosing, I will own that I am glad to know the King does not possess a key to my prison.

"Do your subjects not miss you?" I asked, with restraint. "Sire," I added, grinding my teeth.

"No doubt. But if I left you, then *you* might miss me, and that would be infinitely worse."

"O, but will they not get up to all sorts of mischief while you are away?" I asked hopefully. "Insurrections and mutiny, sire, and other deeds of villainy I cannot think of at the moment?"

"They would not dare," he said indifferently. This seemed so likely to be true that I could think of naught else to say.

"Mayhap I should be going in," I said after a silence during which I watched him sharpening a little silver dagger on a stone.

"But why? If you go you will take the sunshine with you." He straightened up and secreted the fresh-sharpened dagger somewhere on his person. "Come, one so lovely as you could never be so cruel." I noticed that his teeth were pointed, like a dog's. Or a wolf's.

"Yes, well, I must make haste to, ah . . ." I searched my mind for some urgent reason to withdraw. Wash my hair? Embroider a tapestry? My sewing kit was right on my lap as I sat next to the window where he could see it quite well, so that had no merit as an excuse.

"'Tis the Prince," I said unwisely. "I believe that I see him coming."

He whirled on his axis like a dancer. He might be old enough to be my father but I must say he was flexible in the joints.

"You do?"

The little silver dagger flashed out of hiding again.

"Where?"

"O," I said, gesturing vaguely into the forest, "over thereabouts."

"I will go and meet him," the King decided, obviously

pleased to have something to do which would not require him to behave well. "We have much to . . . discuss." And he stepped out of the clearing and melted into the shadows of the trees.

I sighed with relief and then sighed again, this time with resignation. Without meaning to, I had spoken the truth. Prince Edmund of Dorloo was in fact emerging from the forest, leading his horse. The horse was so decorated with braids and bows and tassels that it took all one's ingenuity to guess what 'twas that moved under the mound of finery. The Prince himself was clad in white satin and an elaborate damascened metal breastplate. He looked hot, though not of course so hot as the horse. He doffed his feathered hat and swept a deep bow in my direction.

"Hail, lady."

"'Tis not," I said crossly. I could see the King skulking behind the trees, creeping ever closer to the Prince.

"Not?" the Prince said, assuming his usual expression of someone who has missed a step in the dark.

"'Tis not hailing," I snapped. I simply was not in the mood for the Prince right now, and *he* did not affright me in the slightest.

"The King is right behind you," I added.

"I beg your pardon?"

"TURN AROUND."

"O, well met," said the Prince with a great happy smile, catching sight of the King. Disappointed, the King straightened up and resheathed his dagger.

"Your Royal Highness," he said smoothly, bowing.

The King and the Prince, I must tell you, are both court- ing me. They each swear to be sick with love-longing for me, and so they may be for aught I know. I am of the opin- ion, however, that the sacks of diamonds and gold dust under my bed are as bewitching as my more personal attrac- tions. They are not father and son; they come from neighboring kingdoms. I am to choose between them, which is why I am shut up in this desolate tower.

I have been considering my fate, and the way it appears to me is this: if I agree to marry the Prince, who is young and handsome and somewhat less intelligent than a clod of dirt, he may perchance let me out of this tower before the wedding takes place. 'Twould not occur to him that I might run away when once I had given my word. Which I would do, I assure you, in the winking of an eye.

On the other hand, if I do agree to marry the Prince, the King will simply have the Prince quietly assassinated, and I will end up marrying the King anyway. *He* would never risk losing anything he wanted through foolish trust in a woman's word. No indeed; I shall be treated like the wife of Peter, Peter, Pumpkin Eater, who kept his poor lady in a pumpkin shell, and most uncomfortable *that* must have been. I daresay I'll be walled up in some tower or other un- til the day I die, which could turn out to be a great deal sooner than I might otherwise have expected.

If I agree to marry the King from the first, why then, the Prince is less likely to find a knife between his ribs, which I

5

recognize is a much happier outcome for the Prince. Yet look at what *I* am left with: the old sinner with the concealed weapons and a smile that makes you wonder how, precisely, his first two wives died.

And then I'll be married. Married! At fourteen, in the very flower of mine age! O, I know that many women my age are already married and mothers to boot, but it simply won't do for me.

I am, you see, no pampered Princess, but only a simple Goose Girl with a business to tend and no need of a husband to poke his nose into my affairs. Imagine having to account for your whereabouts to a husband every time you stepped out of the house to relieve yourself behind the gooseberry bush!

Even if I married the Prince and he survived the King's murderous schemes, I don't think I could bear to listen to him going on and *on* about his horse and his armor and his prowess on the field of battle for the rest of my life. Not to mention having to tend his wounds and darn his hose and embroider his coat of arms on every scrap of fabric that we own.

I tried on several occasions to tell my suitors I was too young to marry, but I succeeded only in baffling them both.

"Too young, you say? I am but fifteen summers myself," said the Prince, wrestling with this idea. "Would you have me marry an old woman?" This struck him as being witty. He guffawed and slapped his knee.

"You could not possibly be too young for my liking," said the King, licking his lips unpleasantly. "Young, yes. And tender too, I'll warrant."

I am quite, *quite* certain that I do not wish to marry the King.

I have tried to persuade them to release me by offering them my wealth, but to no avail. The Prince, when I suggested it, fell to one knee, thumped himself mightily on the chest, which, oddly enough, resulted in a muffled twanging sound. He paused to peer inside the breast of his satin tunic and produced a mandolin, which he regarded dubiously for a moment.

"Goose Girl — er, lady," he cried, "you smite me to the soul! I seek your heart and your hand, not your riches."

He struck a bold, discordant note on the mandolin. Several strings flopped loose and a peg flew off over his shoulder.

"Allow me to sing a love song of my own composition in your honor," he said, flinging the crippled mandolin aside and fixing me with the determined eye of a novice performer who sees his audience retreating.

"I thank you, Your Highness, but I must away," I said, and ducked my head back inside.

I knew, of course, how the King would treat my offer even before I made it. He readily promised to allow me to return to my little cottage unmolested, in return for my sacks of treasure. Then, as soon as the servants had loaded them on his horse, he simply rode off, the poor horse staggering under the weight. The next morning he was back again, pretending I had dreamt the whole incident.

"Gold? What gold?" queried His Highness. "Diamonds? What diamonds?"

O, I know very well what you are thinking: "The poor maid must be bedaffled in the brain to entrust all her fortune to a man like that!" But it made no odds to me. There was always more where that came from and I certainly did not want to have to carry those heavy bags with me when I left.

My wealth was a perfect nuisance anyway. All of my gifts were, but the gold dust was the worst. It got into everything: my clothes, my bed, my food. Every morning after the maidservant finished combing and dressing my hair, she had to sweep up piles of glitter off the floor and then shake out my bed linens. Back in the old days when I was a Goose Girl, I used on occasion to find something nasty crawling around on my scalp, but let me assure you that head lice are a rapture and a delight compared with perpetual twenty-four-carat-gold dandruff.

I did not mind the diamonds so much. As they were formed of my own crystallized tears, they only appeared when I wept, and however much my current predicament annoys and distresses me, I never did believe that wailing and puling like an infant does much practical good in the world. It occurs to me, however, that should I be forced to marry the King, he will doubtless see to it that I have good and sufficient cause to fill his treasure rooms up to the very brimful top with the tokens of my grief.

Yet another reason, if aught were needed, to remain a single woman, and I promise you that I shall.

Somehow.

Thus far the best I had managed was to arrange a postponement. I swore by all that was holy that I would choose my husband as soon as I finished sewing my wedding garments. I planned, you see, to be married in a solid gold gown.

"But why?" protested the Prince.

"The gown you are wearing is perfectly adequate," snarled the King, much wroth.

I pointed out that as I was a Goose Girl marrying a royal personage it might be wise for me to be presented to my new subjects as a desirable acquisition, rather than as a liability. The King merely growled irritably but the Prince nodded thoughtfully.

"You mean that if my people could see how rich you are they might not mind you being so low and common?"

I agreed that he had understood my meaning very well.

"What difference does it make *what* your people think?" interrupted the King. "If they don't like it, your remedy is perfectly simple. Drag them out of their homes and chop off their heads in the village square. That's what *I* do."

"No, no," said the Prince. "The Goose Girl — er, the *lady* — has a point. Quite clever of her, actually. We will wait, my lady, until you have sewn your wedding clothes."

And since the tower and the land on which it stood both belonged to the Prince, they waited.

And waited.

Not being an utter fool, I first demanded the finest of gold workers to fashion the gold threads for my gown from the dust collected every morning. Then I found fault with them and sent them away. Once we had run through every goldsmith in both countries, and once it became necessary to admit that I had almost an embarrassingly large quantity of thread, I reluctantly sat down at the loom provided and began to make the cloth.

Naturally, at nightfall I unpicked the work I had done during the day. Well, my friend, what would *you* have done?

Unfortunately, one of the lady's maids acted the spy and caught me at it. After that a servant was required to be at my side both day and night. I didn't much care for that, I can tell you!

Even working as slowly as I dared, the cloth was by and by finally woven, then cut out and pieced together. I was sewing it now, with great sloppy stitches and uneven hems. I am in fact an expert seamstress, but I did not wish to advertise any wifely skills, and, naturally, my clumsy seams kept ripping out and requiring resewing.

Yet however hard I might try to delay it, my wedding day was drawing so near that I could all but smell the meats roasting for the bridal feast.

CHAPTER TWO

The Tale of My Life to the Present Date

SHE LOOKETH AS BUTTER
WOULD NOT MELT IN HER MOUTH.
— JOHN HEYWOOD, *PROVERBS*

My name, I must tell you, is Alexandria Aurora Fortunato, and the reason for all this royal rivalry for my hand — besides, of course, my inexhaustible wealth — is that I am as lovely as the dawn.

You need not laugh; 'tis perfectly true. Back when I was a simple Goose Girl and this calamity first befell me, I used to go down to the duck pond at sunrise to see if 'twas really so. 'Tis not terribly easy to see yourself in a duck pond — your hair hangs down and gets in the way, for one thing — but if anything, I would have to say that I am a great deal lovelier than the dawn. After all, there are dismal dawns and rain-drenched dawns and dawns as cold as charity, but I am always the same: perfectly, flawlessly lovely. Why, for sheer loveliness I'll warrant I could beat the dawn nine times out of ten. And that is without even trying.

I have not always been as lovely as the dawn. Six months ago I was no more lovely than—what shall I say?—a pickled onion. Well, not so *very* bad, perchance, but all knees and elbows and I didn't always keep my face and hair clean. Well, why should I? It never seemed important. The Geese didn't care how often I scrubbed myself, and that pond water is *cold*.

I was only a poor orphan Goose Girl, you see, with no more use for a perfect profile than I had for a slops basin encrusted with emeralds. I *still* have no use for either; it seems to me that the combination of great beauty and great wealth is a monstrous cruel handicap for a girl who simply wants to tend to her own affairs and her own Geese. In the future I shall know precisely what to do if another old beggar woman comes pestering me for a bite to eat while I'm herding my Geese in the high meadow. Will I give her my last crust of bread, like the softhearted, simpleminded dunderpate that I am? No I will not; I'll send her away with a flea in her ear, that's what I'll do. 'Tis said that no good deed ever goes unpunished, and so I am learning to my sorrow.

Before that dreadful old hag saddled me with my three "gifts," which in my opinion were more like a trio of millstones hung around my neck, I was quite alone in the world. My father died before I was born and my mother ten years after. How my father died I cannot say, but 'twas a fever killed my mother. O, but that was a terrible time! She sickened and died, my poor mother, between a dawn and a

12

dusk. Rosy-cheeked and cheerful by morning's first light, she was cold and stark by nightfall.

As she lay dying, my dear mother made me promise to take good care of the Geese. I might sell or eat the ducks whenever I liked, she said, but never the Geese.

"Drive them to pasture in the summer, Daughter, and gather them sweet grasses for winter. You may eat their eggs and make your bed from their feathers, but do not harm them. Treat them well and they will protect you and keep you from want."

I only wept, unable to speak.

"Promise me, Alexandria!"

"As you say, Mother." I bowed my head and kissed her hand. "So shall it be."

Then she died and I, a child of ten years, dug her grave and laid her to rest. The twelve white Geese came and stood around the grave as I shoveled dirt down on my mother's body and I was a little comforted, as though they grieved with me.

Besides my fine flock of ducks and Geese, my mother left me a very small house nestled under the cliffs of Sorrow Mountain and a plot of ground on which stood beehives, fruit trees, and a garden. Every fortnight I would walk the ten miles to the miller's house and trade some eggs or a fat duck for flour to bake my bread. With cloth woven by the miller's wife I occasionally made a featherbed stuffed with duck and goose down, which she then sold in the village for our joint profit. She was an honest woman, the miller's wife, and never tried to cheat me. Unlike her husband, I might add, who was all too apt to lay a thumb heavy as a ham on the scales weighing my flour, if I did not keep an open eye and a chiding tongue in my head. Still, he was not so bad as some I've heard of. Millers were ever rogues and villains and 'tis pure foolishness to expect aught else. I presume they were made that way for some good purpose.

So it came about that I spent three years alone. I lived by my brain and my birds, and let me tell you, 'twas not such a bad life. Before that old beggar woman appeared I had saved up a nice fat little pouchful of money and was happily weighing the advantages of purchasing a she-goat now or a cow in six months' time, when I could afford one.

I was not afraid, living by myself. You see, Geese can be quite fierce with an intruder. If any stranger (which so far as the Geese were concerned meant anybody but me) came within a mile of the place, the Geese all rushed out in a body and screamed and bit and generally chased whoever it was off the premises. And if the intruder had a mind to eat goose pie for dinner that night, why, there was an old musket hanging over the fireplace. Because we lived in such a lonely place, my mother had taught me how to use it, and I was a good shot.

So people generally left me alone. The village was only a mile or two beyond the mill, but I didn't go there often. I didn't think that the village children were either nice or polite. They used to call me a dirty Goose Girl, and sometimes they threw stones. So I simply kept myself to myself.

By and large I was happy. I missed my mother, naturally, but at first I was too busy just surviving to mope much. And later, well, I'd gotten used to it. When I got a craving for company I used to dress the Geese up in skirts I made out of dried grasses and pretend they were neighbors coming to call. The Geese didn't much like it, but I have never been one to stand any nonsense from a goose. Geese, in case you do not know it, are very self-willed animals, stuffed to the brim with conceit and choler. One must be very, very firm with a goose.

So it was that on the day the old beggar woman came I was up in the high meadow, playing at dress-up with the Geese. They were waddling around in circles, flapping their wings and wagging their bottoms, which made all the grass skirts swing like a carillon of giant bells. "Cronk, cronk cronk!" they cried in melancholy voices, and I had to laugh as I tried to herd them over to my make-believe tea party, laid out on a large, flat rock.

As a special touch I had woven a crown of daisies for each bird, and also one for myself, mine being fashioned of wild roses. I was pretending that we were thirteen Princesses sitting down to dine in our ancestral hall.

"My Royal Sisters, please!" I called, trying to sound stern. (In my imaginings, I was of course the eldest sister, she who would one day be Queen.) "Will you not be seated?"

"Well ssso I would if there were anywhere to sssit!" whistled a high-pitched voice right next to my ear. I nearly jumped out of my skin.

But no, 'twas not one of my Geese being saucy. A tiny, incredibly shrunken old woman with just two front teeth, each the size of a tombstone, and a chin and nose so long and so curved that they nearly met in the middle, had appeared literally out of nowhere and was regarding my tea party preparations critically.

"How . . . how do you do?" I asked, very much taken aback, and a little embarrassed to be caught playing at such a baby's game.

"I'm hungry, thankee," she said, looking with burning eyes at the piece of bread I had laid out for my meal.

"I see," I said, dismayed. I was quite hungry myself, and I had been preparing to sup on one scarsly little bit of wheaten loaf alone. However, I said, "Would you like some bread?"

"I would," she said, and snatched the entire piece up and thrust it into her mouth. She gummed it with her mouth open, so that bits of bread fell out onto the ground, where the Geese snapped them up.

"Dry bread always makes me thirsssty," she said. Because of her missing teeth she whistled shrilly as she spoke.

"All I have is water, Grandmother," I said with a sigh, for I was also thirsty after a morning in the hot sun. "But I suppose you'd better have a *little* of that too." If I had any hope that she'd be ashamed of herself and leave some for me, I was disappointed. She even held the flask up over her mouth and shook out the last drops.

"Why, you selfish old—" I began to sputter.

"What do you sssay?" she interrupted, holding up a hand to her ear. "Ssspeak up, girl, I'm a little deaf."

"Nothing," I muttered sullenly. My dear departed mother had brought me up to have the manners of a lady, even though we were poor. I knew that I must show respect to the aged, no matter how boorish and piggy and downright *loathsome* their behavior might be.

"I'll be going, then," she said, thrusting my flask, the only flask I possessed, under her shawl.

"As you wish," I replied between gritted teeth.

She smiled then, her lips curling around her two tombstone teeth, and said, "You're a good girl, and patient with a bad old creature. Very well. When you comb your hair, gold dussst shall fall like rain. When you weep, your tears shall be preciousss diamonds. And you shall be as lovely as the dawn."

"I beg your pard—"

She gave a great cackle of laughter and vanished clean away, taking both my flask and my supper with her. The Geese made a great to-do, flapping and squawking, using this dramatic event as an excuse to wriggle out of their skirts and scatter to all points of the compass.

Once I'd managed to gather the Geese together to herd them back home, I found that the grass skirts they had so thankfully shed had turned to small silken gowns, and the daisy circlets round their white brows were now made of gold and ivory. I am sorry to tell you that I was quite pleased with this discovery at first. If my Geese got golden crowns and silken gowns, what then should I, the kindly maid who had so generously and graciously given my all to a beggar, receive?

I was mad with greed.

Imbecilic, prating fool!

At home again, I at once had a hunt round for my mother's comb. I hadn't actually used it in the past four years, and I couldn't call its exact location to mind.

You might expect that, once I'd found it, it would have taken hours to drag it through the knots and tangles far enough to accumulate even a thimbleful of gold dust, but no. My hair had suddenly grown several feet, developed all sorts of waves and curlicues, and changed color from dirt brown to polished gold. The comb slid through my glittering locks like a fish through water and the gold dust pattered around me like rain, just as the old witch-woman had foretold.

O, but I was a dunce, a simpleton, a most pitiful merry-andrew! I actually sat there and wept tears of joy. And the tears, of course, fell — plink! plink! plink! — as three fat diamonds the size of acorns, into my silk-and-satin-covered lap. For somehow, at some point, my ragged old dress had been turned into the gown of a princess, and my wild-rose crown into a golden tiara topped with great gaudy rubies, red as blood. Dainty little glass slippers sparkled on my feet as well, made of glass beads and solid crystal heels.

Elated, I hoisted the nearest Goose up into my arms and danced her around the house, laughing and singing, the Goose (it was Eugenia, as I recall) struggling wildly as we staggered about, into and out of the fire pit. We knocked the bucket and the ladle off the shelf in the process and badly cracked my best blue bowl. I had to let her go quite soon, of course. Geese are big and heavy and very powerful. I collapsed onto a wooden chest and laughed until I cried diamonds again.

It must have been no more than five days later when I was sitting over my supper of duck eggs fried in grease and deep in rosy dreams of the future, when I heard the blare of trumpets outside my door. You in your wisdom have no doubt guessed that this uproar heralded that very King and that very Prince who now hold me in durance vile.

Each stood in my dooryard with a battalion of soldiers at his back, come to ask me which one I would have in marriage. As I was a subject of the Prince, this naturally made the Prince feel that he had first claim, but being simpleminded, he had let the King talk him into giving me a choice.

Some rotten little beast of a swineherd had spotted me in the high meadow in my princess clothes and crown (I had nothing else to put on save my new gown, though I admit I wore the crown out of sheer vanity and pride), brushing the gold dust out of my hair, and of course after that, 'twas only a matter of hours before everyone in the village heard about it, and a matter of days before the whole countryside for miles around got the news.

Naturally, when I heard their proposals I replied, "Neither one of you, if 'tis all the same to you and of course thank you *very* much." But what was the good of that? I had might as well have been talking to the wind. The Prince looked perplexed and the King looked like cold death, and all the soldiers took a step forward in an extremely menacing manner.

So here am I in the tower, where they can keep a close eye on me while I make up both my wedding garments and my mind. I *must* leave here soon, and yet I don't know where to go even if I do escape. I long to go home, but how can I, looking the way I do and shedding clouds of gold dust and diamonds at every step? Even disguised, the villagers would guess who I was the minute I tried to pay for the common necessities of life with even a pinch of gold dust or the tiniest of diamonds.

I am most dreadfully afraid that my cottage has been looted by those ghastly villagers and that my ducks and Geese are all gobbled up by foxes or wolves by now. I feel so guilty for failing to protect the Geese as my mother commanded. And do you know, I miss them dreadfully. Geese may have their faults, and speaking as someone who has lived intimately with fowl all her life, I'd be the first to admit that they are far from perfect models of gentility. Yet what a comfort it would be to see their peevish, bad-tempered little faces again!

They flew away when the soldiers came, and who can blame them? Not I. I would have gladly flown away myself. Two battalions of heavily armed soldiers, a Prince, and a King was too much to expect them to tackle. I wept when I saw them go and swore I could not be parted from my birds, but to no avail. The sight of the diamonds that poured onto the floor when I cried quite made up the minds of my royal visitors for them.

I gathered up the little gowns and crowns into a sack and brought them along with me. The Geese had always refused to wear them, in any case, and 'twas something to remember them by.

'Twas kind of the Prince, I suppose, to give me Chipper as a sort of compensation for losing my birds. If I were minded to marry and the Prince were less of a dunce — but no, I must be mad to even consider such a notion. He *is* a dunce, and I am *not* minded to marry.

Ah well. If the Geese had been allowed to accompany me here, the King would probably have served them as he did my little Chipper, and with better cause. Any one of my fat and bonny birds would have made a supper fit for a king, which of course is what he is, so perhaps they are better off as they are. 'Tis possible some may have survived.

Yes, I must leave this place. Chipper's death has convinced me. The King is growing bored and my golden gown is nearly finished. I might be able to put the Prince off by going on unpicking my handiwork until the crack of doom, but the King will not wait much longer for my decision. The time to act is now.

Yet how shall I escape? And if I do, where in the wide world shall I go? I do not know.

I am a no-nonsense, practical sort of person and I don't expect that I shall care for adventures — certainly I don't think much of the one I'm in at the moment — but I suppose that from now on adventures will be coming my way whether I like it or not.

CHAPTER THREE

Escape from the Tower

WHEN THE SUN SHINETH, MAKE HAY.
— JOHN HEYWOOD, PROVERBS

They have left the door to my room unbarred. In all the months in which I have been imprisoned here, that has never happened before. In addition, they have left me entirely alone!

The servants, who are also my jailers, have gathered outside to hang laundry in the sunshine and gossip. They are laying wagers on which of my suitors I will accept. The Prince is the popular favorite, since like me they are all his subjects, but at least one of them shares my forebodings about the probable result of my marriage to the Prince.

"What I say is, let that nasty old King have her," the Cook said, her red, beefy bosom heaving with emotion, "else our dear Prince will find reason soon enough to regret it. *If*, that is, he lives long enough to grieve. That King is just as twisty as a little piggie's tail, he is." She nodded her head wisely several times, which made the white wings on her ridiculous headdress flap up and down. "And good riddance

23

anyway," she added with a sniff. "What do we want with a Goose Girl for our Queen?"

Several people disagreed, pointing out the practical value of a Queen, Goose Girl or no, with my particular talents.

"Besides," sighed the boy who polished the shoes and sharpened the knives and tended the fires, "she is the loveliest creature in all the world."

"Handsome is as handsome does," snapped the Cook. "*I* say she's as common as cabbage."

By my oath! I'd never even spoken to the woman. For sheer bounce and bobaunce, I trow I have never heard the like! I happen to have exquisite manners. Indeed, 'twas my refined and aristocratic behavior to that gap-toothed old hag that got me into this predicament in the first place. Mayhap I ought to marry the Cook's beloved Prince just for the pleasure of tweaking the flaps on her silly hat and then sending her packing. But nay, 'twould not be worth it.

I withdrew my head and decided to try a little exploration while they were occupied in discussing my deportment and marital destiny. There was no object in trying to escape through that mob; they were grouped around the only door and would catch me ere I set one foot outside. But if I could not go down, I could go up.

My room was but one story above the ground. However, no one need fear that I would escape through the window. The iron grille affixed to the window frame allowed me to stick my head outside, but no more. By craning my neck

24

back uncomfortably far I could see that the tower was very much taller than the level of my chamber. It should give a good view out over both my own country of Dorloo and the King's country of Gilboa, since it stood almost directly on the border of these two lands. I would climb it and see what I could see. I tucked my golden gown into the bag in which I kept the gowns and crowns belonging to my Geese and bore it along with me. If caught, I could always claim I had been in search of a better light for my sewing.

Three hundred and twenty-six.
Three hundred and twenty-seven.
Three hundred and twenty-eight.

Would there never be an ending to these everlasting steps? My heart felt ready to burst out of my breast; spots swam before my eyes. My legs trembled beneath me like willow wands in the wind.

There were three hundred and thirty-three stone steps up to the top of the tower and much good my long climb did me, as it ended in a dark landing with a flat roof four feet off the floor. I collapsed in a heap, wishing I knew more curse words.

When I had caught my breath I got to my feet again, crouching and holding one hand over my head to shield myself against the stone ceiling. To my surprise, my fingertips discovered that 'twas not stone at all, but wood. Well, of course, there was no particular reason why the tower shouldn't have a wooden roof, but yet it gave me food for thought.

Why build this monstrous tall tower anyway? There were various storage rooms above mine, but it did not need to be anywhere near as tall as 'twas if it afforded no view of the surrounding countryside. There must be a way onto the roof. My fingers groped around in the darkness and eventually found an iron ring. Rejoicing, I put my shoulder to the ceiling and gave a doughty heave.

Ah! The light dazzled my eyes for but a moment. Gathering my skirts together, I climbed up with what haste I was able. To thrust both self and garments through such a small trapdoor was no small feat, and required some kicking and squirming. My Princess gown was a trifle torn, which grieved me some, I will confess. 'Twas the finest dress that ever I had owned and 'twas a crying shame to see it spoilt with rough usage. Still, I managed to struggle out at last onto the roof and that was worth a good deal. I stood up and looked all round.

The tower was much taller than any of the surrounding trees. I felt as if I were looking down from the crow's nest on top of the mast of a ship out at sea. Far, far below was a foaming, tossing green ocean of leaves. And that was all. O, off on the eastern horizon lay some great white objects, but I couldn't tell whether they were clouds or mountains, and in truth it made no odds either way as they were much too far off to signify.

Ah, 'twas a fine, ferly thing, being all alone in that high lonely place! My life in the tower was so *full* of other people. Even when they were not chattering or boasting or laughing or quarreling, they were yet *there* all the time, breathing, thinking, watching. Standing here high over their heads, with naught but blue sky above and green leaves below, I got a queer, hollow feeling inside, as though I were filled right up to the very topmost tip of my head with air and sunlight and silence. A sensation both sad and solitary, and yet it did please me greatly.

Still, from a practical point of view the view was rather depressing. There was no sign of a road or a city or even my little village, which I knew was only a few leagues off. If I were to escape the tower it would mean simply wandering off haphazardly into a wilderness.

Then I heard the rush of wings. Something big and white was coming at me through the air, fast. That Cook, I thought foolishly, flapping up here with her winged head-gear. She's come to fling me off the tower onto the rocks below so that she need never curtsy to a Goose Girl Queen.

But no, 'twas not a Cook, 'twas a Goose. 'Twas one of *my* Geese. In truth, 'twas Alberta. She circled the tower once and then landed.

"Alberta!" I flung my arms around her and squeezed her for all I was worth. "You are not dead! You are not gobbled up by wolves!"

She bit me.

I slapped her back and she honked despairingly.

"By my vertu, Alberta, that hurt. I was merely welcoming you. You might act a bit gladder to see me."

She paid no attention but lifted her head up to look past me at the sky.

"Don't think you're going to fly off again and leave me," I began, becoming thoroughly enraged, "because you're not."

"Honk, honk, honnnk!"

The air around me was filled with great white wings like sails, churning up winds that lifted the skirts of my gown and almost blew away my gold and ruby crown.

"You're here! You're *all* here!"

Eleven white Geese circled the tower

"Ernestina, Lydia-the-Loud, Penelope!" Each goose landed as I called her name and began to preen herself irritably with her bill. "Selena, Simple Sophia, Beatrice-the-Brave, and Dorothea!" Overcome with excitement, I shouted out the last four, "Eugenia, Cassandra Big Foot, Ursula, and my own Little Echo!"

Little Echo landed with a resounding thump (she was never very graceful, Little Echo), and all twelve Geese swiveled their long necks to stare at me. They hissed in unison as though trying to shush me and fixed me with twenty-four accusing little black eyes.

"O, don't be so silly," I said, tossing my head so that my crown slid down over one ear. "They couldn't hear me up here if I shot off a cannon." I leaned over the low parapet cautiously. "Look at them, rattling away like so many wind-mills."

To my amusement, they behaved as though they understood me. The twelve bustled over to peer down at the tiny people far below. As though by magic the worries and tensions of many months lifted off my shoulders and I began to laugh. 'Twas as good as a feast to see and hear them about me again, and they looked so ridiculous, craning their necks anxiously over the parapet in a perfect line! Indeed, 'twas all I could do not to tumble off the tower with laughing. The tower seemed less lonely and my situation less desperate, now that my Geese had returned to me.

As though at a signal, they suddenly rose up into the air. I shrieked in anger and disappointment and cried, "No! Halt! To me! Come back to me, my Geese!" but they paid me no heed.

They circled the tower, once, twice, ever lower with each circuit. To my alarm, I saw riders on horseback enter the clearing. The King and the Prince were drawing near, each hung about with every conceivable weapon that might slay a Goose.

"No," I breathed, "No!" My Geese were flying straight into the crowd of servants at the foot of the tower.

Heads lifted. I saw startled white faces turned up toward my Geese. Ernestina was in the lead and aimed, I now realized, straight at the clothesline where the week's laundry fluttered and snapped in the breeze. She gripped a corner of a fine fat featherbed in her bill and kept going. Alberta, right behind her, snatched up another corner of the featherbed. Lydia-the-Loud and Penelope took the remaining two corners and the four of them whipped it right off the line. Behind them, four more Geese scooped up another featherbed and the last four yet a third.

What in ten kingdoms did they think they were doing? Of what possible use is a featherbed to a Goose?

Up they flew again, proudly bearing their booty to the top of the tower, to me. Ernestina's group sailed down to the tower roof and laid a featherbed out flat before me like a carpet. The others continued to circle over my head with their stolen bedding, watching me, waiting.

The four Geese on the tower stared at me very hard.

"What? What do you want?" I asked, beginning to feel a bit oppressed by their collective stares.

The four glanced at one another and then, as one Goose, advanced upon me, staring all the while with their button-bright, round black eyes.

"Hi there!" I yelped. "Stop that. Bad girls!"

The Geese in the air now landed on the rooftop. They dropped their linens and likewise advanced on me.

"Stop that at once!" I commanded, standing my ground.

All twelve Geese began to hiss like a cauldronful of vipers; their eyes were pinched down and mean.

"What is the *matter* with you?" I demanded.

Dorothea (I think 'twas Dorothea, but since she approached from the rear I was never sure) bit me very hard indeed on the posterior. Clapping a hand to the injured portion of my anatomy, I staggered forward a few paces onto the featherbed.

"You are very, very *bad* birds," I shrieked in outrage. "How dare—"

The Geese scattered. At least, most of them did. Alberta, Ernestine, Penelope, and Lydia-the-Loud returned to their former positions at the corners of the featherbed and rose up into the air, their wings beating, the corners of the featherbed gripped in their bills. I was tipped unceremoniously off my feet and landed with a thump on my poor damaged behind.

"Ow! You shall suffer for this, you rotten—"

Something huge and white blotted out the sky. It was another featherbed, dropped over me by Selena, Simple Sophia, Beatrice-the-Brave, and Ursula. Then, *ploof!* Down came the third featherbed on top of that.

"Ptah, ptah, ptah!" My mouth was filled with featherbed and I could not even begin to express my fury. I struggled helplessly as the featherbed lurched and swayed under me, then flattened and tightened.

I clawed the suffocating folds of linen off my head and roared, "You cannot intimidate ME, I can tell you that, you—"

We were no longer on the tower, but aloft, flying on steady wing beats through the air. Six Geese flew to the left of me, six Geese to the right, and each Goose held a bit of fine featherbed fast tight in her bill.

31

I was being rescued from the tower. And rescued, furthermore, without my having to so much as lift a finger. In short, any further criticism on my part would be a gross discourtesy and entirely uncalled for.

I closed my lips on threats and lamentations and said no more.

CHAPTER FOUR

In Flight

GOOSEY, GOOSEY GANDER,
WHITHER DO YOU WANDER?
— NURSERY RHYME

An arrow flew past my nose. The sunlight caught and gilded it as it crested and began its earthbound journey. I reached out my hand and took it from the air. There seemed to be all the time in the world to do this, but in truth my hand must have moved swiftly. I caught the arrow just as it pierced Little Echo's left wing. She faltered a moment and then beat on.

"Little Echo!" I cried, withdrawing the arrow. "Are you injured?"

She didn't look at me but went on flying steadily. Yet on the upbeat I could see a spreading stain of scarlet on her left shoulder, the one closest to me. Several more arrows sped past, but none found a mark.

"Stop!" I commanded. The Geese exchanged glances, rolled their eyes heavenward, and went on, ignoring me.

"O, very well," I said, a little embarrassed. "I suppose you

33

cannot actually stop in the middle of the air. But Little Echo *must* have her wing bound."

I cautiously inched my way over to the edge of the featherbed. Looking down as best I could through goose bodies, I saw with relief that we were out of range of any more arrows. The tower was already beginning to look small and toylike in the distance. My Geese, though larger and whiter than their wild cousins, must have been only a few generations removed from them, for they were strong flyers and bore me boldly onward. In spite of Little Echo's danger my heart lifted up and I rejoiced. I laughed aloud.

"O my brave and clever ones!" I shouted into the wind. "We are away!"

Then, when she was least expecting it, I threw an arm over Little Echo's back. She squawked in alarm, but I pulled her struggling, protesting body onto the cloth. The expressions of the other Geese grew a bit tense as they coped with all this tugging and jerking.

"Now lie still, Little Echo!" I said sternly. "Are you not ashamed of yourself?"

Mayhap she *was* ashamed, but if so, she hid it well. At any rate, she must have realized the futility of resistance, for at length she quieted down and lay there looking up at me apprehensively.

"I must wash the blood off," I mused. "But how? I have no water here."

Keeping a firm hand on Little Echo to prevent her escape, I took another peek over the edge of the featherbed. This was not easy, as one was quite likely to be smitten in the face by an uplifting Goose wing. What I did see did not look encouraging. We were flying over the King's country of Gilboa now and 'twas much more populous than my own country of Dorloo. I was looking for a solitary lake or pond at which we might land so that I might bathe Little Echo's wound. Each and every single source of water, from the largest to the smallest, seemed to have a cluster of human habitations ringing it.

When we had flown some time without finding a safe place to land, I sat back up and thought. Where could I find water in the middle of the sky? Water, I reminded myself, comes from the sky in the shape of rain. I looked up. There were a quantity of low, puffy clouds above us, some not so very far away. I knew not what clouds might be made of, but did they contain water — why then, I meant to have some for Little Echo's shoulder.

I leaned forward and tapped Ernestina on the back. Her eyes flicked toward me.

"Go higher," I said loudly, gesturing in case she didn't understand me. "I wish to go up."

I wriggled over to the other front corner of the feather-bed, where Alberta labored, and repeated the request.

"'Tis for Little Echo that I ask it," I explained, feeling a trifle foolish as I did so. I am not in the habit of explaining the whys and wherefores of my actions to a gaggle of Geese,

35

but this was not my element. On earth I was the sovereign ruler of my household, but here in the upper air the Geese were at home and I was not. I might choose to issue commands which they might choose not to obey. And what I would do in that circumstance I knew not, to be quite candid with you.

With powerful strokes of their wings, we began to rise. The other Geese grasped our change in direction and soon we were headed straight into a small dark cloud.

Clouds are not what you might imagine them to be from seeing them on the ground. I used to think, ignorant girl as I was, that I should like a gown cut from a cloud. How fine and white and soft 'twould be! I no longer desire this. 'Twould not be decent, to speak truly. Why, a cloud does not seem to be anything but a great mass of mist or steam, and a girl dressed in a cloud gown might as well be walking about in her shift and naught else.

However, there is water in a cloud. Upon my honor I do believe that clouds are nothing *but* water which for some reason has chosen to go very small and then wander aimlessly across the vault of heaven instead of raining down to earth as it ought, where it could be of some use.

Within moments everything save the Geese had become thoroughly damp. The water rolled right off the Geese, as I had observed it to do during a rainstorm, but both I and the bedding were drenched.

I was now glad to see that the bag containing my golden

wedding gown had come along with us, as it also contained a little pair of silver scissors. I realized with regret that my Princess gown would have to be at least partially sacrificed to bind up Little Echo's injury. Tearing the featherbeds would mean losing their stuffing, and my golden gown seemed to be the wrong sort of material for making into bandages. I therefore cut my hem into several long strips.

"What cannot be cured must be endured," I sighed. "'Twas ripped already, besides."

I instructed my Geese to drop back down into the sunlight that we might dry off and warm up.

Obediently, they dropped with such a lurch that my inner organs seemed like to fly right out through my lips. I did not offer any remark, however, but waited in silence until my gizzards reseated themselves. I would not have Ernestina and Alberta (ever the leaders of the flock) thinking that I had not the intestinal fortitude for this sort of travel.

Little Echo's wound was not so dreadful as I had at first feared. My hand had robbed the arrow of the force to penetrate very far into the muscle, and it had missed the bone altogether.

She lay still on my lap while I tended her. Often and often I had doctored the Geese in the past, and this one in particular was quite accustomed to my ministrations. Little Echo, for all her small size, was both a pest and a tease, fond of sneaking up on the others and stealing a choice tidbit from under their bills, or nipping them on the knees, or ducking them in the pond. She was well and truly bitten for her pains and several times had needed bandaging after some mischievous act.

So accustomed was I to scolding her as I bound her up that now I found myself abusing her heedlessness from habit. Then I recollected that she was injured, not through some bit of nonsense in the duck pond or our own home meadow, but in the act of rescuing me from the lewd embraces of a kingly cutthroat or, in the Prince's case, an imperial ass. I bit my lip and abruptly fell silent.

Once Little Echo was cleaned and bandaged I released her, the while keeping a wary eye on her. She was ever a wild little thing and, even though she had acted the part of a heroine today, I did not trust her.

Now at last I was able to sit and look about me and take pleasure in the ride. What I saw, however, was little more than a great many pumping white wings. The featherbed sagged under my weight and Little Echo's and, when I was sitting erect, the wings of the Geese were at my eye level. Yet there was an intense blue dome of sky above, and after a time a crescent moon rose over the edge of the featherbed.

The sky slowly darkened and the stars began to show, pale and lonely. I soon understood why my Geese had procured for me not only the featherbed which was my chariot, but two others. 'Twas cold here in the sky when once the sun was gone.

Suddenly I thought to wonder where we were going.

"Where," I inquired, "are we going?"

None of the Geese responded. Even could they have spoken with a human voice, their bills were fully occupied with the featherbed.

"Do you not grow tired?" I asked. "Would you not like to rest for a time?"

In truth, I myself was becoming a bit bored. And hungry. Nor was I accustomed to sitting in one position for such a time. How I longed to stand up and stretch my limbs!

"We shall have to stop somewhere for the night," I argued, as the birds flew steadily on. I knew that although wild geese sometimes fly at night during long migrations, my own domestic birds never did. And never had they flown such a distance before, let alone with the burden of Little Echo and myself.

"I pray you," I added, as my left leg suddenly cramped.

However, my request was ignored. We sailed silently on through the velvet-black sky. I pulled the featherbeds closer about myself, shivering, and rubbed my calf ruefully. I would not ask again.

It came into my mind that we had lost height, and I did not think that it was because we were landing, but rather because they had not the strength to keep us up so high so long. There was desperation now in their weary wing beats.

Whither did we wander in the night sky, and why?

I struggled to keep my eyes open. The labor of this flight was none of mine, yet I would not be carried like a helpless child, nor yet like some bundle of goods going to market. Though I could do naught to aid us in our journey, I sat up very straight and pinched my arm until the diamonds trickled down my cheeks. Little Echo, less proud, slept at my knee.

The land below us was dark and without feature now, but the scent of earth and leaf informed me that we traveled ever closer to the treetops. Would these demented fowls persevere, steadily sinking into calamity? Would the dawn's first light discover our mangled bodies, all to-brosten in a poor, pitiable pile at the roots of some mighty oak tree?

No sooner had these queries formed in my brain than the featherbed dropped like a rock. In certes, I would not be kept in suspense for much longer.

"Alas!" I cried. "My doom is come upon me!"

Thump! Thumpathumpa thump!

Trees, tall grasses, and several large boulders hurtled by.

"O woe! O! O! OW!"

We had landed.

CHAPTER FIVE

The Cottage in the Wood

TWO HEADS ARE BETTER THAN ONE.
— JOHN HEYWOOD, PROVERBS

The house in the clearing where we had landed might have been our very own, had we returned to it after ten weary years of exile. The winter winds and snows had gripped it hard and twisted it out of true. The door had fallen in and the thatched roof showed great dark gaps where the spring rains had penetrated for many a year.

A duck pond there was, as like to ours as is a reflection. An overgrown apple orchard like ours was there as well, and what mayhap was once a tidy vegetable garden, now a jungle of tall, tough weeds.

Aye, and also were there two grave markers shining dully in the moonlight by the edge of the wood. They were the image of the one which stood at the head of my mother's grave. Uneasily, I noticed that the graves had been disturbed. They gaped evilly open before me.

"O, Alexandria Aurora Fortunato," I hear you cry, you who are my friend and listen so patiently to all my tale, "art thou then such a blithering bumblebrain? Did this not teach

41

you prudence? Could there be a worse omen than an open grave?"

I did not care. I cared only that the evening was now blacker than the coal pits of Hades and that here before me was shelter, of sorts, for the night. You may call me a knotty-pated niddlenoddle if you will, and worse, but I refused to go one step further that night.

I merely shuddered a little and turned my back on the ominous little hollows. Tonight I meant to sleep within walls, even though it be on a dirt floor. Those six long months in the tower had accustomed me to sleeping soft in silks and satins, and I did not fancy stones in my bed and a root for a pillow.

The Geese were lying in a dispirited heap upon the ground where we had landed, much exhausted. No wonder in that! However, when they spied me walking toward the cottage, they bestirred themselves. At first I thought that they were hurrying to enter the cottage themselves, but soon saw that they meant to prevent me from doing so.

"N-a-a-a, n-ah, n-ah!" they whickered anxiously, pressing closer as I tried to push my way through them.

"Shoo! Shoo, now. Get away from the door, girls," I cried. "I wish to go inside and see what is what."

Still they would not budge, but blocked the way in the most maddening manner. Much vexed, I found a stout stick and began to drive them away. I was not happy about the way they were trying to run things on this journey.

42

As I prodded and pushed and poked with my stick they began to give way. They did not like it, but they moved away from the door.

"N-n-a-ay! Nay, nay, nay!" they cried piteously as they retreated before my stick.

What, I began to wonder, would I do if their protestations were justified? Verily, there was a stench of corruption and death within. Mayhap some fierce animal denned in this deserted house. Or perchance a robber gang slumbered on the other side of the ruined door. My courage almost failed me as I thought these thoughts, but I would have none of that. I was the leader of this expedition and 'twas for me to determine where we would spend the night. I took a deep breath and stepped over the threshold into the cottage.

It took some little time for my eyes to adjust to the greater darkness inside the hut. Indeed, to speak true, 'twas too pitch-black to see much of anything. However, I moved cautiously around the room (like our old home, the cottage was only one room large), poking my stick into every corner. This did not take overmuch time, as there was nary a stick of furniture in the place. A large metal object there was, like a big cooking pot, a great many oddly shaped bowls lying about, some store of cloth as it might be rags or bags or discarded clothing, much filth and debris on the floor, and not one thing else that I could find.

I sighed with relief and called to my girls, "Look you here, you silly ninnies, there is naught in this place to fear.

We shall sleep secure tonight, away from the fearsome beasts of the forest."

They would not come.

"Nay, nay, ne-e-e-h!"

"Come, my foolish ones! See? You may escape through the hole in the roof if any danger threatens, while I must stay behind to perish. 'Tis quite safe for *you*!"

They did come into the cottage, but only to gather about me and try to herd me out again. Seeing, however, that they were all within, I made shift to push the door shut and rammed it up tight against the frame with the big cooking pot.

"Faugh! What an odor there is here, to be sure! Tomorrow we must have a grand clearing out of all this claptrap and clutter underfoot."

I spread out two of the featherbeds, retaining one for a covering, and curled up quite comfortably.

"There!" I said brightly. "Is this not pleasant? Here are we, snug and protected 'gainst any evil of the night, be it spirit or flesh. How say you now, my Geese?"

"Doom, doom, doom," they replied. "O, doom!"

"Hush your noise," I snapped. And paying no more mind to the frights and flutterations of my flock, I rolled over and slept.

"Whoooo's been aproppin' of our *elegant* kicked-down door?"

'Twas barely light in the cottage, and a monstrous black

44

shape hovered over me. Immediately I reached out on both sides of my body to confirm that my Geese were at hand and uninjured. I felt naught but featherbeds. In my dreaming memory I retained the sound of rushing wings and knew that they were gone.

Instead of the Geese I hoped to see, I beheld a human skull with the top half sawn off. Indeed, there appeared to be many of these gruesome objects laying about. These, then, were the oddly shaped bowls I had felt in the dark.

"Whoooo's been ashiftin' of our great black cauldron?"

There were *two* huge black shapes hovering over me.

"And whoooo's been asleepin' on our *bonny* bone-strewn floor?"

To be accurate, there were now three huge black shapes hovering over me.

"Git up, girl, thy doom is done," pronounced the first shape.

"Dyin' time is nigh," agreed the second shape.

The third said nothing, but pulled a simply enormous butcher knife out of its voluminous black gown and licked its skinny lips.

"O, fie upon it all!" I muttered under my breath. Not another one of *those*. Why did everyone save myself seem to be carrying lethal weapons on their person?

"Good morrowtide, madam," I said, scrambling to my feet and curtsying to the first shape, which I now perceived to be that of an Ogress with two heads, each more hideous than the other. "To — to both of you, that is. And to you

45

ladies also." Here I curtsied to the other Ogresses. "As you say, I have taken the liberty of sleeping in your charming though somewhat derelict cottage while you were away. I am most glad indeed to meet you that I may express my gratitude and find some way to show my thankf—"

"Hish up, ye bladderskate," said the first Ogress, shaking both heads until her noses wobbled. "Mine earbones ache with thy drasty speech. Don't talk so much."

"Certainly not. I shouldn't dream of it," I said, peeping around the room out of the corners of my eyes. The Geese were gone. I could only hope that they were indeed gone through the hole in the roof and not outside trussed up for the cooking pot. "I am much aghast at the thought of causing your earbones any discomfort whatsoever. In truth," I went on, "I trust you will not mind my mentioning it, but you look most lamentably tired. You have been up all night, I imagine, hexing people and souring the milk of your neighbors' cows."

"How dast ye, missy?" demanded the first Ogress, but the other two made some snorting noises behind their filthy, horny hands which I interpreted as laughter.

"*Very* tiring work, hexing people," I said sympathetically. "Or so my old Auntie Ogress used to tell me when she came in after a hard night's ill-wishing. And then I used to comb her hair for her and trim her beard and make her a lovely cup of "—here I cast about in my mind to try to think of what ingredients might be available which would make a lovely cup of anything—"hot nettle tea," I concluded tri-

46

umphantly, having observed these stinging plants growing in the old vegetable garden.

"Oooo," observed the second Ogress thoughtfully.

"Never mind all that," roared the first Ogress, whose one head was bearded while the other was bald. "Iffen we don't kill and eat this juicy little dumpling, what, pray, are we going to do for dinner?"

"Why you poor *things*!" I exclaimed. "Have you not had anything to eat? By your leave, dear ladies, I should be honored to prepare a meal for you if you would only let me. 'Twill not be aught luxurious, you understand, since I am not at home with my things around me, but 'twill be enough to chase the wolves from your innards."

If they were fools enough to let me go off foraging for food in the wood, that would be the last they would ever see of *me*.

"If we kill her, we shall have to cook her ourselves," observed the second Ogress, who possessed coarse hair sprouting in random tufts all over her body, including a luxuriant growth from a large mole at the end of her nose, and skin the color of a blade of new grass.

"Aye, and she's bound to be a better cook nor either of *you* are," argued the third Ogress, standing with arms akimbo, her hands on her hips. This would not have seemed so queer had her arms not been twice as long as they should be, so that she looked like a windmill or a great black bird of prey about to take flight.

The two-headed Ogress was clearly puzzling over a

method whereby she could force me to cook myself so as to save them the trouble. I decided to behave as though the matter were settled.

"Excellent! Have you by any chance got a basket or anything of that sort in which to put my gleanings? No? Never mind, I shall use my skirt. And now, of your charity, I must be going out and about, you know, so as to get us a bite to eat."

"She'll run away!" shrilled the third Ogress. "Let us tie her up, Tessa!"

"That's all very well, Lucinda, but with what?"

They looked about themselves, as though they thought that a stout rope might materialize out of nowhere, neatly coiled up on the hearth.

"There is naught here, I tell ye," said the bald head of the two-headed Tessa. "We got to kill her or she'll run away." The bald head appeared to be the more talkative of the two heads, but now and then the bearded one chimed in with some remark.

"Do you know," I said brightly, "I believe I have just the thing here in my bag. Do you see? It is a spool of golden thread from my sewing kit. Tie it round my waist if you don't trust me." I intended, of course, to untie it as soon as I was out of sight.

"What good is that?" growled Tessa. "She'll only untie it as soon as she's out of sight."

'Twas becoming clearer every moment that Tessa was a perfect pest.

"*I know*," said Lucinda. "Tie her up by her hair."

I frowned. My hair, while long and luxuriant, was no more than four feet in length. I wouldn't be able to roam far.

"By her hair?" protested Nellie. "What good would that do?"

Tessa rolled all four of her eyes. "Nellie, y'blockhead, any fool can see the maid's got enchanted hair."

Lucinda stretched out one of her prodigiously long arms and grasped a sizeable hank of my hair in her grubby hand.

"All ye gots to do is sweet-talk it a bit, I trow." She ruminated on the hair for a moment, spit on the ground, and then pronounced:

> "O yeller Hair,
> Most goluptious fair,
> N'er have I seen
> A fleece more fitten fer a queen.
> Why, I expect it grieves ye somethin' dretful—"

"Git to the point," interjected Tessa.

"Keep yer hair on," said Lucinda. Nellie snorted. Lucinda went on, "Enchanted things is real conceited. Ye gots to lay it on thick." She closed her eyes and proceeded.

> "O bee-yootiful Hair,
> So daintevous rare—"

"We can't sit here all day while you sing love songs to that there hair," said Tessa. She reached out and grabbed a large lock of my hair with such energy that my head came with it.

"Listen to me, hair," said Tessa. "You heard them praises like Lucinda said. What we wants now is fer you to grow an' grow an' grow, but never break. You hear me?" She waggled the lock of hair threateningly.

"Git over here, missy." Tessa gave a great tug on my hair and dragged me staggering over to the caved-in door. There she knotted my hair around an iron ring attached to the door frame.

"Now then, missy, git thee gone!" and she landed a clout with her huge fist right in the center of my back that sent me flying.

"And mind ye bring back somethin' fitten to eat!" she bawled.

I ran.

By very good luck, the door was agape where the Ogresses had entered. My legs whirled round and round like the spokes of a wheel. My shoulder blades fair ached with the power of Tessa's blow.

Free! I thought to myself as I helplessly hastened up hill and down dale, through bramble and bracken. For I *must* be free of the Ogresses now. I had run far, far longer than the length of my hair away from them by now. Gradually I gained control of my nether limbs and at length stopped and turned around.

My golden hair streamed out in a broad ribbon back, back, back to the iron ring in the doorway.

I gasped at the treachery of it all. "Most perfidious, villainous hair!" I cried. "How come you to play me so false? Wicked! You are wicked, I say!" I tugged on the hair with both hands, but it did not yield; nay, the only result was a positive shower of gold dust.

"Ooo!" I shrieked, overcome with wrath. "Thou nest of vipers! Thou mangy mass of beaten straw! I'll take a scissors to thee, see if I do not," I said.

But my threats were in vain, as my sewing kit was left long behind me in the cottage. I was obliged to mutter as I trudged onward and my temper cooled, "Faithless hair, do you not know that you bring about your own ruination as well as mine? If I die, so then does my hair." Yet the hair did not so much as tremble in the breeze.

There was naught to do but go onward and look for food. As I did not wish to become entangled amongst the trees, I stopped to look about me, trying to plan my path. Much to my relief, I spied a great quantity of those rushes named cattails growing in a marshy area beyond the duck pond. These, I knew, had tubers which would keep body and soul together for many a day. I need not return empty-handed save for a mess of nettles.

You may be sure I also had a good look around for my Geese as well, but nary a feather did I see.

"Really," I muttered aloud, "a worthless lot you twelve are. You might have stayed to defend me."

"Honk!"

I smiled. They were here, then, and not far away.

"Forgive me," I called softly. "My heart rejoices me that you flew away, else you might be bound as securely as I. Nay, 'tis better as 'tis. Do not show yourselves. I shall hope to free myself in the next few days."

"Whoooo's that you're atalkin' to, missy?" shouted one of the Ogresses, who evidently had hearing as sharp as an owl's.

"O, no one," I shouted back, airily. "Not a single soul."

"Well, hesh up, then. My word," she bellowed, "what a creetur you are for talkin'. And hurry up with them vittles."

In silence, I bent my head to the task and did my best to comply.

CHAPTER SIX

In Which I Become
a Servant to the Ogresses

A NEW BROOM SWEEPS CLEAN.
— PROVERB

*W*hat I say is, we ought to keep her," said Lucinda, reclining at her ease on my featherbeds while I ruined my good sewing scissors cutting her huge horny toenails. "She be a regular marvel, she do. Bet this old house hain't been so clean and shinin' like since it were built. Looks real nice." She looked around at the swept hearth, the roaring fire, and the wildflowers on the windowsill. "Pretty little thing, too."

"And so say I," muttered Nellie drowsily, hugging her distended stomach by the fire. "She do be a better cook nor any o' us. I hain't eat so good in fifty years. Hey, Tessa? Meal weren't bad, were it?"

I awaited Tessa's verdict with some trepidation. 'Twas she, I felt sure, who would decide my fate.

"No meat," said Tessa's bald pate briefly. Her bearded head drew back its lips in a grimace, displaying a large set of yellowed teeth.

"Still and all, we can't expect the maid to bring down a stag with her bare hands, can we? Not while she's tied by the hair, nohow. 'Tain't reasonable," Nellie said.

"Humph," said Tessa.

"Do I understand, madam," I said, "that you are offering me a position in this household?"

"What y'*should* understand, and what y'*don't* understand, is that yer to keep yer trap shut up tight," Tessa snapped.

"I only ask because I was wondering what my wages might be," I explained.

"O, wages, is it? I'll wage you, I will," snarled Tessa.

"Yes, thank you, I realize that. I'd just like to know what the wages would *be*."

"Why you —!" Tessa turned so purple that I feared for her health. "How so be it if we don't kill you? How would that be for wages?"

"Well, frankly, my lady, I was hoping for a bit more," I said.

"Blast and stummergast thee, if I don't —"

"O, don't be such an old wart, Tessa," interrupted Lucinda. "Don't see why we need t'untie her until we're ready to let her go, but she could have that necklace thing, couldn't she? *We* never use it."

"How dare you even mention the jewels, y'mutton-headed hag? Rubies the size of hen's eggs, and ye want to hand them over to any pretty face that wanders by."

"'Tis a small enough thing to keep the maid sweet tempered. Words, ye know," Lucinda said, winking significantly at Tessa, "do be as free as air."

Tessa's two heads turned to commune silently with each other for a moment, then back to Lucinda. "Hunh," said the bearded head, but no further objections were made.

Lucinda said, "Don't ye worry, little missy." She winked again at Tessa. "Ye'll git yer wages when ye go."

And so I became a servant to the Ogresses.

I cared nothing for the promised necklace. I had only asked for wages to distract Tessa from the question of meatless meals. In any case, a promise is easy enough to give when you have no intention of honoring it. I was tied by the hair still, however much I might argue and complain. If the Ogresses tired of my services and the meals I supplied, why, I was a tethered meal, requiring only to be killed and cooked.

'Tis dreadful inconvenient, being tied by the hair. I must confess that the hair did at least have the common decency to grow or shrink depending upon my distance from the iron ring on the post, so that we were not all tripping over leagues of the stuff when I worked about the house. Still, there is no getting away from the fact that 'twas a most villainous nuisance. The further I got from the cottage the heavier it grew to drag along behind me, until I could scarce move forward for the weight of it. Then too, it was always getting wound round trees and caught up in bramble bushes, and 'twas more tedious than I can tell, unwinding and unpicking myself everywhere I went.

One might expect that the hair would grow dull with dirt and filled with burrs, but it never did. Nay, it shone like the rising sun and curled as sweetly as a grapevine tendril. So I had not even the excuse of washing it as a pretext for being untied.

I was unable to cut it, as I had threatened. When I returned that first day I found that my scissors had been removed from my sewing kit, though all else remained. No other tool had I to sever the hair, since the butcher's knife I used for cooking must be begged from Lucinda and promptly returned.

Nor was I able privily and by stealth to untie the hair. Indeed, it did not appear to be tied at all, but grew in a continuous circle round the iron ring. In my desperation I tried biting through it, but 'twas as tough as gold wires.

After the first morning, I neither saw nor heard my own dearling Geese anywhere. The only sign that I had not lost them altogether was that each day a white feather, weighted down with a small white pebble, appeared on a certain large rock near the cottage. Next to them was always a Goose egg, which helped me in my quest for food. Each day I put into my sewing bag the feather and pebble and also the broken halves of the Goose egg after we had eaten it.

As the days went by the Ogresses became more and more impatient with the meals I served, growing nostalgic for their former diet.

"O for a haunch of child meat," said Tessa, sighing wistfully and picking over as nice a stew of wild mushrooms, garlic, and coltsfoot as you could meet in a day's march. "A good little boy of no more than six years, f'rinstance, round and sweet as a butterball. What wouldn't I give?"

"*Much* too rich," I said. "You'd be awake all the livelong day with indigestion and you know it. And if you *did* manage to snatch a few winks, I have no doubt you would keep everyone else awake with your bad dreams."

"O pshaw!" she responded, but she held her peace, merely glancing resentfully at her sisters, who were snorting and poking one another and nodding in agreement.

"Terrible, she be, after a meal of fresh child-flesh. The moans and groans are enough to break your heart. Still," said Nellie wistfully, "it do be a treat, now and then. I miss it, I will confess." She raised a dripping handful of stew to her mouth and eyed me speculatively as it trickled down her chin.

Apparently they'd eaten up all the inhabitants of the deserted little village nearby. They were now obliged to find their dinner in the village graveyard, and even this source of protein was giving out at last. The occasional unwary traveler such as myself was a real windfall.

I did my best to satisfy their cravings for flesh, indeed I did. I contrived to bring back a few birds and small beasts for the cook pot with a catapult made from a thong of leather I found lying about (best not to wonder whither the leather came from!) and a forked stick.

'Twould not do for much longer. Even I was growing weary of boiled cattail tubers *every* evening. Still, I did my best to keep the upper hand as long as I could.

"Nellie, watch how you are holding that bowl," I scolded. I had transformed some of the sawed-off skulls into bowls, but they were awkward to manage, being full of holes, imperfectly stopped up. "You are slopping stew *all* down your front. Now I'll have to wash that dress again and you won't have a thing to wear until it's dry."

"Awww," she said, ruefully inspecting her dress. "It hain't so dirty. Why do y'got to wash it fer?"

"Y'know what's happenin' here, don't yer?" demanded Tessa. "She's reformin' of us, that's what she be doin'. Next thing y'know, *she'll* be the one runnin' the show." Tessa snorted. "Y'notice that? Whooo be it what issues the orders around here lately? Me, what's the eldest of a long and proud lineage? Or her, what's a servant and what should of been our dinner?"

"Her," agreed Nellie.

Tessa made an unlovely noise deep in both of her throats. Her four eyes followed me as I moved about the room.

I could not feel easy in my mind about my future prospects in this household. Besides which, some of my duties were rather repellent to a person of fastidious tastes. 'Twas as if I were playing nursemaid to a trio of gigantic children with particularly nasty personal habits. The number of times I had to break up quarrels over some old bone, or prevent Lucinda from pulling Nellie's hair out by the roots! Well, you simply would not believe me if I were to tell you.

Of course any one of the three could have crushed me like a beetle underfoot. Tessa in particular was at least eight feet tall and five feet wide, while I was rather slender and delicate of frame, though wiry and strong after years of fending for myself.

O my friend, I tell thee that there were nights when I did dream of naught but Tessa's teeth. *Both* sets of them.

'Twas the morning of the twelfth day that the Ogresses caught yet another unhappy traveler. I knew it to be the twelfth day because I had eleven white feathers, eleven white pebbles, and twenty-two eggshell halves in my sewing bag, and had not yet gone out to forage for food, which is when I normally found them.

I got up before dawn as usual and tidied the cottage, sweeping the usual gold dust outside, where I carefully dispersed it over the dooryard dirt. I was most vigilant in performing this duty, and in dusting every surface of the cottage, for I did not wish the Ogresses to know any more about my gifts than I could help. You might wonder that I did not offer my wealth in exchange for my freedom, but if you do so wonder, kindly recall the result of my previous attempts in this direction.

Once every gleaming grain of gold was gone, I began cooking our great meal of the day as usual. Suddenly I heard a tremendous tumult coming up the path: roars and moans, shrieks and groans. There came a sound of heavy bodies falling about into the shrubbery.

I rushed to the doorway to see what was the matter. This was a bit difficult to tell at first. There was such a confusion of gigantic arms and legs and massive chests and hips that I couldn't immediately decide what I was looking at, and the fact that the sun was not yet up did not help. Presently, however, I determined that it was the three Ogresses wrestling with a large black sack which was in violent motion.

"Hold his feet, ye! Nellie!"

"Ugh!"

Nellie was toppled like a tree in a tempest as the black sack suddenly jackknifed.

"Hold him, can't ye? Lucinda, make y'self useful."

Lucinda wound her enormously long arms around and around the sack like a snake, and Tessa settled the issue by sitting down on both Lucinda and sack at once.

"Gerroff! Gerroffuvit!" came Lucinda's muffled roar from underneath her sister's weight. Tessa did not move, however, but simply sat there. Both of her heads grinned ferociously.

I could see a rather elegant, well-polished boot protruding from under Lucinda's body, a boot which did not belong to Lucinda; obviously this was not some woodland creature which they had snared for the pot.

I opened my mouth to order them to immediately release whatever unfortunate soul they had imprisoned in that sack, when I caught the expression, identically reproduced, on each of Tessa's twin faces. Two sets of eyes glinted wolfishly, and two tongues darted out of two mouths in an expression of naked greed. But 'twas *me* she was looking at, not the sack.

Now was not the moment to exert my precarious authority.

I closed my mouth and then reopened it.

"Excellent," I said cheerfully. "You've brought home some dinner, I see. How clever of you all."

CHAPTER SEVEN

The Misfortunate Knight

IT IS A DEAR COLLOP THAT IS
CUT OUT OF THY OWN FLESH.
— JOHN HEYWOOD, *PROVERBS*

Tessa was most grievously disappointed, I could see. Trying to make them let the man in the sack go might quite easily have been fatal for me, and Tessa knew it. Lucinda and Nellie were simply not in the mood to be told that ladies never eat human flesh. They had, with considerable difficulty and after many days of nearly meatless meals, caught themselves an unfortunate knight whose skill and valor had not been equal to the brute force and size of the three Ogresses.

They now intended to cook him and eat him, and if I chose to object, why then I was welcome to join the benighted traveler in the pot.

"Drag him inside and tie him up with the golden thread while we decide what to do with him," I instructed.

"What do ye mean, decide what we do with him?" demanded Tessa. "We be agoin' to kill him, that's what we be agoin' to do with him. Hand me that knife, Lucinda."

But Lucinda, being underneath Tessa and with her arms wrapped several times around the man in the sack, was unable to comply.

I took the opportunity to walk over and inspect what I could see of the sack. He appeared to be wearing very little armor; apparently his errand had not been of a warlike nature. He was no merchant, however. I could see plain as day that his coat of arms was embroidered into his surcoat, though most of it was obscured by the sack. This was of no moment, as I was ignorant of the devices of the noble houses in this part of the world.

"The gentleman appears to be a bit underfed," I remarked, leaning down to pinch his leg. "Most likely he has been wandering in the woods for days without a bite to eat." I shook my head. "I fear he will cook up lean and stringy."

Nellie ceased her wild dance and eyed me suspiciously. There was a mutinous look on her face as she said, "What of it? He'll taste a mort better nor a mess of old cattail roots, I warrant."

I nodded, as though much struck by her observation. "Verily you speak true. But wait!" I cried, as Nellie turned a greedy face toward the sack and Tessa began to cautiously ease herself off Lucinda. "I have a notion. Why should we not fatten him up for a few days before we eat him? We could give *him* the cattail roots, you know. There wouldn't be any need to cook up anything special for *him*."

"Well . . ." said Nellie.

"Now lissen here, missy," said Tessa.

"I'm hungry *now*," Nellie whined.

"Mmmph!" said Lucinda.

"Tessa, you have to let Lucinda up in order to get the knife, you know," I pointed out. "And the moment you do *that* he'll make a run for it. You will have to tie him up."

In truth, I doubted that the man could have gotten away, not blinded as he was by the sack. Mercifully, even both of Tessa's heads put together had not the wit to see this. They turned on me a look of pure dislike and then the bald one barked, "Nellie! Get me the golden thread that her is allus agoin' on about."

I swiftly produced the great skein of golden thread and handed it to Nellie. In a trice Tessa had bound the sack sufficiently for both Lucinda and Tessa to get off it. The sack did not stir throughout all of this. Mayhap he was half suffocated and crushed, poor fellow. Or wholly suffocated and crushed, perchance.

"G'me the knife, Lucinda," commanded Tessa as soon as Lucinda had scrambled to her feet.

"Whoof!" said Lucinda, one hand to her chest. "Wait a bit, can't ye? I be fair scrunched."

"Lucinda," said Nellie, "What d'you think we should do? Eat it now or fatten it up like Alexandria says?"

"Now! Now! I do be as empty as a gourd." And she whipped out the knife and flourished it in the air.

I stared at the polished boot and thought furiously. Within moments the gentleman belonging to that boot would be no more than various cuts of meat.

"What, pray," I said suddenly, "has become of his horse?" Surely that boot wouldn't look so elegant had he come here on foot.

The three Ogresses stopped and looked at each other. The sack emitted a low groan. He was not dead, then.

"What did we do with the horse, Tessa?"

"Don't remember."

"Well, I do," said Nellie. "I brought it along of us and laid it down behind the cottage since it were dead, or next thing to it. I figgered we could have it later. Fer dessert, like."

The sack groaned again.

"Most shrewd of you, Nellie," I said. I grieved for the man in the sack, but what else was there to be done? We still lived and the horse did not.

"We shall have a delicious horsemeat stew for our dinner. *Much* better than waiting for this tough meat here to cook. Why, 'twould be hours before he was fit to eat." I hastily excused myself in order to go and inspect our next meal.

All I could see behind the cottage was what appeared to be a mountain of cloth, metal, and leather. This puzzled me mightily until I realized that what I was looking at was the saddle and fitments of a royal charger. I nearly groaned aloud. For never, surely, could there have been *two* horses so festooned and bedecked in all this world. 'Twas the Prince's horse, without a doubt.

I had been thinking of the man in the sack as a potential ally. But nay, quite the contrary; I should now be saddled with this silly simpkin in a situation of most dreadful peril and uncertainty. Was there ever anything so misfortunate?

I drew near the dead horse and began to strip off the trappings.

"Alas, noble beast!" I sighed. "'Tis indeed a pity to see thee lying here, about to be carved up into cutlets."

Something moved under the pile of gear. I hastily backed away as the mound heaved mightily and struggled to stand. The horse had not been killed but merely stunned. Most likely it had been nearly crushed under all that equipment. Now that the weight had been removed, 'twas recovering from its swoon. It could do no more than struggle, however, for the poor animal's legs were bound together and it could not rise. At length it lay still and looked up at me, eyes rolling in terror.

I scowled back. Dead, the horse had solved a problem. Alive, he became one.

"O, very well, I suppose I must set you free," I said. "But what I shall feed to the Ogresses I simply do not know." I bent to untie its bonds. "Lie still, Sir Horse," I commanded. "I've no desire to be kicked for my pains. Now off you go, and right speedily, for 'tis death to linger in this place."

Obediently, the horse kicked up its heels and vanished into the gloom of the forest without so much as a grateful glance in my direction.

When once it had departed I sat myself down and began to lament my lot in earnest, for what would happen to us when the Ogresses had discovered the loss of the horse? The stew I had prepared was made of naught save a few old roots and leaves. What, *what*, was there to hand that would give it a flavor of meat? I looked despairingly about me.

In certes, we were doomed.

My eye fell upon the leather saddle at my feet. Might the Ogresses not, after so long on a vegetable diet, have forgotten the taste and texture of horseflesh . . . ?

Ah, well. Naught venture, naught have. I would do what I could.

'Twas not the best stew I have eaten.

Verily, I believe 'twas the *worst* stew that ever did pass my lips. Before I carried the saddle inside to cook it, I pounded it betwixt two boulders until my arms ached, both in order to make it more tender and to disguise its shape somewhat.

Once inside I cut it up into pieces, none larger than a pea. Then I added it to the meal I had already prepared and boiled it over the fire until the vegetables lost their shape and the water cooked away and the Ogresses bellowed for their meal.

They ate it. They were not best pleased, but they ate it.

"Toughest ol' horse I ever did eat," muttered Tessa, choking on a lump of leather. "Must have spent its whole life eatin' thistles and tree bark."

Anxious to encourage this train of thought, I quickly agreed. "Indeed," I said, resolutely chewing away at a chunk until my jaws did ache most cruelly, "'twas almost a kindness to put the poor beast out of its misery. Shame on you, sirrah," I said to the man in the sack, "to treat a helpless animal in so scandalous a fashion!"

The man in the sack appeared to attempt a lengthy, indignant rebuttal, but was hampered by having a mouthful of sack and eventually subsided.

After much grumbling, the meal was consumed and the Ogresses lay down for their day's rest. Seeing this, I made so bold as to ask for my sewing scissors of Lucinda.

Instantly suspicious, she demanded, "What be that to the likes of ye?"

I might have replied that I merely wished to catch sight of my own property, but I had no desire to antagonize.

"I want to cut the top of the sack off," I replied.

"What fer?"

"I must feed him, madam. And I can't do that if his mouth is covered with a sack."

"Ugh," Lucinda grunted. "See to it that ye give 'em right back, then," and she withdrew from her bosom my silver scissors.

As I leant down to cut the sack it occurred to me that the poor man might react poorly to having scissors brandished in his face, particularly when he could not see who was doing it.

"I'm going to cut the sack off your face," I said in a low, clear voice. "Do not move or I shall cut you by mistake." The sack became very still.

With a few adroit snips of my scissors, I freed the man's

face and head and swiftly thrust the scissors under a small stack of firewood which lay nearby.

"Alas!" I sighed when I saw the man's face. My hopes were dashed; 'twas the Prince, his very own self.

"Alas, indeed, my lady," he began jabbering as soon as he saw who addressed him. "I am come, at great risk and jeopardy to my life, that very life which is so precious to my people, to set you free, and now—" Suddenly his eyes rounded with horror and his jaw dropped agape.

"'Twas you, then, who spake with such a—such a ghastly *relish* of fattening me, ME! up for the table? Indeed, it was! Why, 'twas your very voice!" His eye fell upon the human skulls converted to bowls and drinking vessels. He gasped.

"My horse!" he cried out in anguish. "Thou unnatural, depraved female! What hast thou done with my poor horse?"

Tessa, I noted from the corner of my eye, had raised up one of her heads and was observing our discourse. I was therefore unable to speak kindly or give him aught of comfort.

I gestured at the steaming cauldron on the fire.

"As you see, my lord, we have eaten him."

He shut his eyes and groaned. "To think! To think that 'twas once the dearest wish of my heart to make this maid my wife! This, then, is the She who should have been mother of my heir, the first lady of the land! O that I had—"

Here he paused perforce, as I thrust a dipper of cattail

mush into his open mouth. I did not wish the Ogresses to know that the Prince and I were acquainted if I could prevent it.

"Monstrous, I say!" he roared, spattering mush all over me. "Do you wish to choke me with your vile potions, Night Hag? Night Hag thou art! I wonder I did never guess that you flew away in order to join these, your hideous sisters."

"Whooo do ye be callin' hideous?" demanded Nellie, beginning to swell like a toad.

This also roused up Tessa's other head. "Shut yer trap or I'll kill ye, here and now, and no more wastin' of good food on ye."

"O, very well, if you say so," he said, silenced by the direct threat. Not, however, for long. "But," he muttered peevishly in a tone which, while lower, was perfectly audible, "I consider that I have been treated very ill, and now to be *eaten* for my pains while attempting to rescue this wicked, ill-bred — Ow! Why do you pinch me, Goose Girl? Do I not suffer enough?"

Really, I began to be sorry I had cut the top of the sack off.

I thrust the dipper of cattail mush back into his mouth, as much to quiet him as to nourish him. He sipped in silence, only murmuring in a puzzled voice, "Your hair has grown somewhat since I saw you last, has it not?" as his eyes followed the curving line of my tresses out to the door. I did not trouble myself to answer.

Gradually the Ogresses slumped back down onto the

featherbeds once again, and soon the sound of snoring filled the room. Yet still I dared not speak frankly to the Prince; they slept lightly and I feared would wake at the slightest sound. At length I finished feeding the Prince — I wished him well-fed when we made our escape — and stealthily reached my hand under the stack of firewood for the scissors.

"What are you doing, Goose Girl?" demanded the Prince aloud. "What is that which you have in your hand? Scissors?"

By my vertu, if I could have smote him dead on the spot I would have.

Lucinda woke up immediately. "The scissors!" she cried aloud. "Alexandria, g'me those scissors right this very minute."

"In certes, madam," I said, grinding my teeth. "I did but forget."

Casting such an evil eye on the Prince that he visibly recoiled, I got up and restored the scissors to Lucinda.

"Now be off with ye and leave us to sleep. I want some o' that nettle tea when I wake, y'hear?"

"You'll not go off and leave me alone with them, will you, Goose Girl?" asked the Prince in a much lower voice.

"I'faith, I will," I said coldly.

"I beg pardon for calling you a Night Hag," he said humbly, but I was gone, trailing my golden tresses behind me.

CHAPTER EIGHT

In Which I Remain Tied by the Hair

FAST BIND, FAST FIND.
—JOHN HEYWOOD, *PROVERBS*

"*O* my Geese," I called out over the valley as loudly as I dared. "Come to me now in my need."

Naught stirred below or above me. I had toiled up to the top of this hill overlooking the cottage, hoping to see something of my birds. I could easily trace my own steps for these past many hours; the long yellow band of my hair zigzagged back and forth betwixt hill and fen, cottage and creek, like a golden road between the trees. But I saw no living thing else that moved.

"'Tis I, Alexandria Aurora Fortunato, who summons thee," I added.

Not so much as a glimmer of white feathers.

"For the sake of the love we bear one another and for the sake of my dear dead mother who harbored and succored thee and spared thy lives each and every Christmastide, e'en when we were faint with hunger and a hot Goose dinner would have been very Heaven itself, I command thee to come to me at once," I shouted.

Naught but a still, hot blue sky hanging over silent woods.

"O Hades," said I, and kicked a tree full hard with my glass slipper. 'Twas remarkably painful. Under my breath I mumbled, "Useless, featherbrained, asinine, half-witted . . ."

'Twas energy thrown away, and I had no more time. I must get back to the cottage and prepare the evening meal before the Ogresses awoke and ate the Prince for want of aught else.

"I am leaving," I shouted. "I am going away, most likely to my death. So I shall not see thee again." I gulped a trifle and my voice cracked as I cried, "Fare thee well, my Geese, and may thy wings carry thee to a place of safety and bountiful grasses and, and—" I broke off, unable to go on. I turned and stumbled down the hill, tears flowing freely down my face. Diamonds tinkled and clinked on the rocks and stones in my path all the way down the slope to the cottage.

I could not enter the cottage at once, but must first re-tread my path through the valley, unweaving my hair from the countryside. This wearisome task completed, I paused ere I reached the cottage and packed half of my day's gleanings in the Prince's saddlebags, which I had found with the rest of the horse's fittings.

The saddlebags already contained a number of useful things, such as a lovely little bow and quiverful of arrows, a silver cup, a cooking pot, a tinderbox, and two fine blankets. Yet one more item was there, an object which I in my quiet life had never before laid eyes upon, yet which I recognized at first glance. 'Twas a book.

Verily, I shuddered with almost superstitious dread when I drew it forth, for there is a strange force in the written word. They who command it command great power.

My mother almost never spoke about her past life before she came to our cottage in the wood, howe'er I might tease or plead. Yet once she let slip the fact that in former times she had owned not one, but many, many of these precious objects, mayhap even so many as five. Thus did I discover, more truly than had she boasted of jewels and silver and gold, that I came from greatness. When the village children threw stones and called me a dirty Goose Girl, I remembered my mother's great store of knowledge and laughed them to scorn.

Indeed, my mother had most kindly begun to teach me my letters, even though I was but a Goose Girl with no need for book learning, when she saw that I wished it. I grieve to say that she died ere I could advance any further in my education than this. I am therefore in a position to tell you that the writing on the outside of the book contained one *A*, two *B*'s, two *E*'s, and a number of other letters with which I am not familiar, as my scholarship does not extend beyond the letter *G*. Still, 'tis not every Goose Girl who knows her *E*'s from her *B*'s, I can tell you that!

I restored the book to the Prince's saddlebags after conquering a brief and ignoble impulse to hide it amongst my own things. 'Tis a matter of wonder to me that the Prince should own this erudite object, for surely such a one as he could not comprehend it, could he?

The saddlebags I modified so that they could be slung round the shoulders of a human, rather than attached to the rear of a saddle, for we would be our own steeds on this journey.

Lamentably, the saddlebags did not contain that which I most coveted: a knife. How I did long for a sweet little blade, bright as the sun and as sharp as pain! Mayhap the Prince's was lost in the struggle (I looked most carefully round and about on the ground), or mayhap Lucinda had simply taken charge of it and any sword there might have been, as she did all cutting tools. I could not believe that even the Prince would have set forth into the wilderness armed only with his wits, such as they were.

I had found the twelfth white feather under the usual pebble in the usual place, next to the egg, and that had given me hope that I would catch sight of my birds as I made my preparations. All that day I had been scanning the sky and the underbrush, calling out their names one by one, my hopes slowly dwindling as the hours went by. My trip to the top of the hill had been a last, forlorn attempt to call them to me before returning to the cottage. Later it would be too late. 'Twas risky even now; the Ogresses would be stirring soon and preparing to go out for the night. His Highness and I would leave under cover of darkness while my Geese slept, and the need for secrecy and silence would seal our lips.

The fire glowed red in the dimly lit cottage as I let myself in through the tumbledown door. Nothing moved, not even the Prince. Anxiously I studied his form for a sign that he still lived, that the Ogresses had not slain him in my absence. Yes, his breast moved gently; he merely slept. That was as it should be. He would need the rest if he was to attempt a long journey tonight. I only wished I could have done the same.

Briskly I began preparing the usual cattail roots, along with a hot nettle drink. Once the cattails were well boiled and mashed, I approached the Prince, thinking to stir him up for his evening meal. I had intended to touch him lightly on the shoulder to rouse him; 'twould be a dreadful enough awakening without my adding to the horror. But my eye caught the gleam of firelight reflecting off a slitted eyeball over in a dark corner. 'Twas one of Tessa's heads watching me while the other slept. She was as suspicious as ever and waiting for me to show the slightest weakness.

I drew back my foot and kicked the Prince in the stomach, hard enough to make an audible thump. He groaned and jerked in pain.

"Your dinner, my lord," I said demurely. I pushed him into a sitting position and prepared to feed him.

"What have I ever done to you, Goose Girl," demanded the Prince between gritted teeth, "that you should serve me in this manner?"

This question was too much for me to resist. I bent forward and breathed in his ear. "Only locked me up in a tower for six months, that is all, my lord."

"But—" He began on a high note of outrage, then was silenced when I inserted the dipper of cattail mush into his mouth.

In a louder voice I said, "I am hungry, and weary of boiled roots, sire."

"You are a perfectly dreadful young woman," he observed bleakly.

I shrugged and pushed the ladle back into his mouth. My point had been made and I saw no need for further playacting.

"Enough!" Tessa rose from her dark corner, and her sisters stirred. "Don't give it all to him. I do be hungry."

"Aye. I be hungersome too," said Nellie, yawning and stretching.

"I be absolutely *famished*," said Lucinda, propping herself up on one elbow and staring ravenously at the Prince. "I be so hungry I could eat—"

"A horse!" I concluded cheerfully, holding out sticks with steaming lumps of boiled and grilled leather from the horse's bridle and reins impaled upon them. "And so you shall!"

"O pshaw!" muttered Lucinda, but she took her skewer of meat and began slowly munching on it. The others followed suit and I began to bustle about, tidying.

"And so, my dear mistresses," I said casually as I swept

the hearth, "what are your plans for tonight? Do you think of trying the next village down the valley? 'Twould be a blessing to find a new source of meat. This one," I poked at the Prince with the broom handle, "will not last forever, you know."

"That be a real good idea," said Tessa unexpectedly. "Why don't we do that, girls?"

"But, Tessa, I don't want to go so far," objected Lucinda. "My bones ache so tonight that I can scarce stand upright."

"Let's have a dig in the graveyard, I say," said Nellie. "There might be somethin' there we missed and we wouldn't have to walk so far."

"Shut up yer traps," snarled Tessa. "I said we're agoin' down the valley and so we're agoin' down the valley."

After much grumbling and complaining it was agreed that the trio would go down the valley in search of the next unsuspecting village they might feed from. Inwardly I rejoiced; aught that took them far away was to our advantage. All appeared to be shaping well for my plans.

And yet . . . 'twas so little like Tessa to approve of a suggestion of mine. I had hoped to win Lucinda and Nellie to the idea of new worlds to conquer; never had I expected to find Tessa on my side. My heart thumped in my chest as I waved farewell in the doorway, watching the three sisters lumbering away into the woods.

Once out of sight, I whirled about, my eyes scanning the cottage for anything that might sever my hair.

"A knife, a knife, I would give all the wealth of the Indies for a knife!" I muttered as I rummaged among the skulls and tibias that littered the corners. "An ax! A hatchet, a scythe, a rusty old hoe! Is there naught here that will serve my will?"

The Prince drew back, aghast. "You . . . you would not murder me, Goose Girl?"

I glanced malignantly at him, remembering how he had deprived me of my sewing scissors through his o'erweening stupidity. But yet I must reassure him and gain his trust ere we fled through the forest.

Shaking my head, I said, "Nay, I'll do no harm to you, Prince. Indeed, I shall do what I can to save your valuable neck, if only you will most faithfully promise to obey me in all things." I fixed him with a fierce stare, which mayhap did little to embolden him. "Will you?"

"I—I," he hesitated. "Do you mean in *all* things?"

"'Tis what I said, is it not?"

"O, but—"

"You do not trust me. I do not blame you. But what chances, my lord, do you think you have if I go away and leave you alone here tonight?"

"We-ll—" He eyed me dubiously.

"Promise, or I shall go this moment." 'Twas of course all bluff on my part, as I had not yet the means to cut my hair.

"Yes, but wait," he begged. "For how long must I obey you in all things?"

I debated. 'Twas a fair question. "Until we reach home

and safety, or until I release you, whichever comes first," I replied at length.

He nodded slowly. "Very well."

"And when we do reach our home, you must promise me that you will never press me by force of arms, or by any other means, to marry you, and that you will defend to the death my right to remain single so long as I wish."

"O, in certes I will," he said, with some emphasis. "I shouldn't think of pressing you to marry me again. 'Tis for the best, no doubt, that you remain unwed. Marriage, I am told, is ever an uncertain estate and some are not best suited to it by temperament or training." He flinched as I smashed a human skull on the cauldron and then tried sawing at my hair with the resultant sharp edge. "You, mayhap, are one of these, Goose Girl. In point of fact," he went on, "I doubt I shall ever marry, myself. My judgment is not what it should be. I do not know when I have ever been so mistaken in anyone before. You seemed quite a *nice* maid if somewhat —"

"O do hush!" I said, abandoning the smashed skull. "Let me untie you. We must away as soon as possible and you will be ill prepared for walking until you have shaken up your limbs awhile."

I did so and then returned to my primary task: finding a way to free my hair. Could I, I wondered, pluck out each hair from my head until I was as bald as an egg? 'Twould take eons to do, I feared.

"Goose Girl," said the Prince, who had been wandering aimlessly about, easing his cramped limbs, "did you know that your hair goes all the way over here to this iron ring on the doorpost?"

I ignored him. Could I *burn* it off?

"I *said*, Goose Girl, did you know that —"

"Yes! Yes, Your Highness, I did know that my hair goes all the way over there to the iron ring on the doorpost! How, in the name of all that is reasonable, could I *not* know such a thing?"

"Well, you need not be so vexed at my asking," said the Prince, offended. "I merely thought 'twas a remarkable fact, and so I remarked upon it. You cannot blame me for that, can you?"

I crossed my eyes at him and stuck out my tongue. He quailed before me and then rallied.

"You may make what fearsome faces at me that you please, Goose Girl, and I may not resent them, for I have promised my obedience to your will. But tell me, pray, how are we to leave this place if you are tied by the hair?"

"A most excellent question, Your Highness," I said through gritted teeth. "I confess I do not know. Have you any suggestions, perchance?"

The Prince appeared pleased at having his opinion sought.

"I should think that some cutting tool, such as a knife or a scissors . . ." He broke off, looking somewhat embarrassed. "I do not believe that I have any suggestions at this moment in time. However, allow me to consider the matter and I will do my best to produce some."

"I thank you, sire." Then, knowing 'twas futile, I asked, "What happened to your own blades? Have you anything about you?"

He shook his head mournfully. "My sword was taken by the two-headed lady, and my knife by the one with the arms. I regret to say that I am without a blade of any sort."

We both sat in silence for a few moments.

"How did your hair come to be so bound?" he asked at last.

A surge of irritation washed over me. Could the fool not be still and let me think? I was about to say so when it occurred to me that my mind was as barren as a barley field in winter. I had no ideas whatsoever. Why should I not tell him what he asked? 'Twould pass the time until my approaching death as well as aught else.

I told him. He wanted all the details, which I gave in a resigned tone of voice. When I had done, we sat again in silence for some time, I trying to bestir myself to tell him to flee for his life and leave me to my fate.

"Why," he said finally, "could you not do the same, Goose Girl?"

"What do you mean?" I asked drearily, wondering exactly how the Ogresses would choose to kill me.

"Could you not ask the hair to let go? Politely, of course. You would have to be polite. But could you not ask?"

CHAPTER NINE

On the Run

IT HURTETH NOT THE TONGUE
TO GIVE FAIR WORDS.
— JOHN HEYWOOD, PROVERBS

"O beauteous hair, most daintevous rare . . ."

I swallowed. 'Twas bitter gall and wormwood to be forced to flatter my own treasonous hair. I nearly asked the Prince to do it, but in the unlikely event that his idea had any effect, I could not bear to allow his lordship to gain mastery over my hair when I had it not. I would most humbly petition my hair though it choked me.

I could not remember exactly what Lucinda had said, but it had not seemed to be a set rhyme. I began again, making up my own words.

> "Never was there
> Beauty so rare,
> As my hair!"

"Do you know," I interrupted myself, "I shall feel a perfect fool if this does not work."

"Go on, go on," said the Prince. I made a grimace of distaste, but reluctantly continued:

> "Angels in air
> Have locks less fair,
> Than my hair!"

"'Twas most excellent well said, that bit," the Prince whispered. "Now apologize."

"For what?" I demanded, outraged.

"Hush!" He flapped his arms at me. "Do not undo the good you have done. Did you not tell me that you spoke harshly to your tresses?"

"'Twas entirely justified."

"Grovel, Goose Girl, if you wish to be free."

"O very well," I said. Was it my imagination, or was the Prince enjoying this?

> "Grieved I should be [I snarled]
> Did I hurt thee,
> O my hair!"

"Now get down on your knees," suggested the Prince.

I ignored him. I would make my request and have an end, for good or ill.

> "Let me go free,
> I do beg thee,
> Good, kind hair!"

I could not resist pointing out an obvious fact in my last stanza:

> "Please hear my prayer;
> One fate we share,
> O *wise* hair!"

Reflect upon *that* awhile, O my hair!

Nary a thing happened. I stood there gawking at the loop of hair like a loblolly on a lamppost for what seemed a lifetime. Then I sank, groaning, to the ground.

"Woe is me," I mourned. I dropped my head into my hands. "O woe is me, for I fear that I must die."

A soft swishing sound and a gentle brush 'gainst my cheeks and arms could not rouse me from my grief. I huddled miserably against the door frame, waiting for eternity.

After some time, I heard the Prince clear his throat. I must order him to leave me, for the night was wearing on.

"I do beg your pardon, Goose Girl. It pains me to interrupt your reverie, but ought we not to be going? You might not have noticed, but the night is wearing on."

"You go, sire," I said without opening my eyes. "There is no reason for you to perish too. You are unfettered; go." A large diamond rolled down my cheek and into my lap.

"But Goose Girl," he protested. "I know that I did most faithfully promise to do all you command; however, I must say that under the circumstances I really do not see—"

"O, wilt thou go!" I scrambled to my feet and shook my

fist under his nose. "Thou gomeril! Thou goop!" He stepped back several paces. "Thou art like to drive me mad! Go! Go! Go!" I gave him a hearty shove with my hands.

"I pray you, mercy," said the Prince, offended. "If that is your wish, then I must." He bowed so low that he nearly toppled over. "I will hope to hear you overtaking me, for the night is long and the woods are dark and deep. I speak merely out of concern for *your* welfare."

I watched him retreat, anger vanquishing fear at least for the moment. I shook my head, unbelieving that so much folly could exist in one human brain.

And as I shook my head I felt a sensation I had not known these past twelve days. My hair was tickling my arms. I wheeled about. Yea, verily, I was bound no longer. I was as free as a dandelion seed, floating on the wind.

"Wait! Your Highness! Wait for me!"

I had to return to get my possessions, but soon we were hurrying through the dark valley, he laden with the saddle-bags and I with my sewing kit. The Prince had eyed this bag with what I fancied was the light of criticism in his eye. 'Twas true that crowns and gowns and suchlike fripperies were of little use in the wilderness, but I had worked so hard on the cursed golden dress that I could not bear to part with it, nor could I bear to leave the tiny gowns and tiaras belonging to my Geese to be despoiled by the Ogresses. O, perchance the feathers, pebbles, and eggshells were of small value, but yet they were the only mementos of my Geese that I had left.

For some time I was too grateful for my freedom to do aught but rejoice in the beauty of the night and the pleasure of being abroad in it. A full moon rode the crest of the hill and the wood was streaked with silvery light. Yet after a while I began to be a mite uneasy.

"Halt, my lord," I said at last. "Do you hear aught?"

"'Tis only the wind in the trees, Goose Girl," said the Prince.

"But there is no wind," I replied, and I felt a growing disquiet.

We walked on for a time.

"Hist!" I cried in a harsh whisper, gripping the Prince's forearm. "My lord, do you not hear a rustling in the leaves?"

"'Tis only a blackbird dropping down to its nest, Goose Girl."

"But blackbirds do not fly at night," I said, and O, how I longed for a bright little knife in my hand.

We walked on through the moonlit forest and our shadows fled before us.

"Nay, my lord," I cried out in a fever of fear, "you *must* hear that roaring, rushing sound behind us!"

"'Tis only the stream roaring and rushing o'er the rocks in its path, Goose Girl," said the Prince in the tone of voice used to soothe toothless babes.

"But the stream is before us, and not behind us." I halted

and remained rooted to the spot, scanning the darkness. "Beware, my lord! See where they come!"

Tessa, Lucinda, and Nellie emerged from the shadowy wood. All four faces wore terrible, lunatic grins.

"Well, if it hain't our faithful servant Alexandria!" cried Tessa. Her bearded head was festooned with moss and bracken, and her bald head shone dimly in the moonlight. "What do ye be doin', wanderin' in the wildwoods so forlorn? 'Tis a darksome dangerous place fer a lady like ye be." All her eyes glowed yellow.

"Come back, Alexandria," said Lucinda. Ropes of glistening saliva hung from her exposed fangs. "Ye've left without yer wages. We gots to give ye yer wages, missy."

"GIVE US BACK OUR MEAT!" roared Nellie, pounding herself on her chest.

I groped for something, anything, to say that would avert their rage and greed.

"I . . . I—" I faltered. There was naught that I could say. The situation had gone far beyond words. And we had no weapons! I thrust my hand into my sewing kit, searching for the memory of a pair of scissors. My hand closed on a mass of goose feathers. Feathers! Of what avail was that to us?

Lucinda pulled something out of the bosom of her dress. I flinched, expecting to see the butcher knife. 'Twas not, however, a knife, but something that glinted bloodred in the cold light of the moon. She swung it, temptingly, before me.

"See, missy? 'Tis yer wages what we promised. Just you

come over here and git it." She advanced, fixing me with a glittering eye.

Wildly I looked about for something to throw at her. Nothing; there was nothing.

She stepped closer.

"Cease and desist, hag," cried the Prince. He leveled his bow at Lucinda. Ah! the bow and arrows. I had forgotten them.

"Go your ways and leave us to go ours or I shall shoot."

She came on, still dangling the necklace before her.

There was a twanging noise next my ear, then a thunk! as the arrow landed squarely in Lucinda's chest. Twang! And another arrow joined its brother.

She smiled, drawing her lips up high so that we could see her gums and count each and every tooth. Then she plucked the arrows one after another from her bosom, as if they were brambles caught in her clothing, and flung them away. Onward she came.

"She can't do that," protested the Prince.

"She *is* doing that," I pointed out.

"Then—why then, *you* do something, Goose Girl," croaked the Prince in a strangled voice.

"I—"

The three Ogresses stepped closer. Lucinda stretched out one hand with the ruby necklace in it, and with the other she made a snatch at me, her monstrous long arm seeming to stretch yet longer as it swung nearer.

I shrieked. Stupidly, pointlessly, I threw the feathers I held in my hand at her.

Instantly the world utterly changed. From black darkness, all became white. A bitter wind screamed about the Prince and me, and the temperature plummeted from warm and tender June to icy January. The Ogresses were nowhere to be seen, but a ruby necklace with great gaudy stones as big as hens' eggs fell at my feet into a mound of the cold whiteness.

I turned to the Prince, who was standing behind me with his mouth agape. He swallowed.

"That was most, uh, resourceful of you, Goose Girl," he said, quite respectfully. He stooped and picked up the necklace. Handing it to me with a bow, he continued, "As much as I should like to understand what you did to bring about this really very surprising event, it occurs to me — ought we not to retreat while those ladies are otherwise occupied?"

"Gaaah—" I responded cleverly. I turned back and gazed once again at the white devastation before me. Now that I looked again, I realized that 'twas a great mountain of snow that had reared itself up betwixt ourselves and the Ogresses when I flung the goose feathers.

"You — I . . ." I gabbled. With an effort I pulled myself together. "You are in the right, sire. We must go, and as quickly as we may. They are powerful and long-limbed, and will overtake us if we do not hurry."

Which indeed we did. We picked up our heels and ran.

"I protest," huffed the Prince when we had slowed to an

energetic trot, "I am struck dumb with amazement."

"That, sire," I observed grimly, "will be the day."

"I [puff, puff] do not understand you, Goose Girl."

"'Tis of no consequence, sire."

"Very well. But will you not tell me how you effected that remarkable occurrence?"

"I must save my breath to make our escape, my lord," I gasped.

"Very well." He sounded sulky, but was himself soon too much occupied in breathing to spare energy for speech.

"I must—" I wheezed at length. "I must halt. I can go no further for the moment." I staggered into a tree and sat down.

We had gained the mouth of the Ogresses' valley and sat on a hill looking down upon it. The strange white mountain of snow gleamed in the moonlight 'gainst the inky forest about it.

"Fie upon it," I muttered when I had regained my breath.

For there they were, three black blots on the white field, coming closer and closer by the instant.

"They outran my horse Bucephalus," the Prince said. "They will be with us in a trice. We must go."

"Wait!" I cried. "I cannot! Not for some moments. I must rest."

"Then I must hope that you have something else in that bag that will save our skins, Goose Girl." And he sat down with a resigned air.

But what could that be? I groped about in the bag. A

Goose crown? But 'twas not mine to fling away. A gown, either mine or one belonging to the Geese? I shook my head in despair. How could I tell?

I drew forth the ruby necklace. I held it aloft, appraising it. "Perchance this will do," I said. "They may give up and go home when they regain their treasure."

The Prince frowned. "Nay, Goose Girl. Coming from a humble station in life, you may think that those are merely pretty red stones, but I assure you that they are very fine rubies. I dare say they are worth a king's ransom, always assuming that the king in question be ruler of a not overly prosperous nation or mayhap provided with a great many sons or otherwise—"

"Your point is, sire?" I demanded a bit testily.

"'Twould be folly to throw it away heedlessly," he concluded with admirable brevity. The Ogresses had drawn so near that I could make out the two heads of Tessa, the dreadfully long arms of Lucinda, and Nellie's tufts of hair.

"You are quite right, my lord, in believing that, coming as I do from a humbler sphere, I cannot value this bauble as you do. 'Tis rubbish to me indeed, compared with our lives."

"Try something else first," he suggested. "You may always throw the necklace if all else fails."

"What, pray tell, do you wish me to throw?" I could see the hairs growing from Nellie's nose mole. I had braided them for her last night and I perceived that the braid was coming undone.

The Prince viewed the contents of my bag.

"Why, look at these pretty little crowns," he said with pleasure. "So neatly made, and so very tiny. They might almost be made for fairies —"

"They approach, my lord. What would you have me throw?"

"Not these little dresses. One can't really get much distance, throwing a dress. Here, I see, is your golden wedding gown. I never entirely believed that you were exerting yourself to the *fullest* extent to finish that, you know."

"Your Highness —"

"Throw these," he said at last.

He held out the broken eggshells which my Geese had left for me, each half shaped like a large white cup. I sighed. 'Twas true enough that these would look like no more than refuse to the Prince, but I misliked losing them, for they had once most intimately belonged to my Geese. There was, however, no time.

I stood up and flung them at the Ogresses.

This time there was a vast blue expanse betwixt us, a blue that was nearly black in the moonlight. I could still see them, far off on the other side of the blueness. The cups of the Goose eggs had become a great lake, upon the shores of which we stood, they on one side, we on the other. The tiny figures of the Ogresses began to jump up and down in transports of rage.

The Prince regarded this circumstance with considerable self-satisfaction.

"An excellent choice, do you not think, Goose Girl? I

doubt that they can swim, not unless they are witches as well as Ogresses, and I don't suppose that that is likely, though of course all things are possible. I make no claims to be an expert in the matter, you know."

'Twas now well advanced toward dawn, and the sky had turned a pearl gray in anticipation of sunrise. I could see that the Ogresses, now recovered from their temper tantrums, were moving purposefully about.

"Nay, my lord," I said, "I do not suppose that they can swim, but evidently they can build a raft."

"O, curses!" he cried, and then looked mortified. "My apologies, Goose Girl," he said. "Even though you are only a common Goose Girl and a bloodthirsty, bad-tempered, horse-devouring one at that, 'twas wrong of me to use bad language in your presence. Will you not forgive me?"

"I'll forgive you anything, sire," I said briefly, "provided you help me over yonder fallen tree. They are coming. It must be sorcery of some sort, for I do not know how else a raft may be made so swiftly."

This time we had only run for a few scant minutes when we could hear their craft beaching on the near shore, and within a few more we could hear the Ogresses themselves approaching fast and furious through the bushes and bracken behind us.

We had no leisure to stop this time.

The Prince gasped out, "You must throw something else, Goose Girl."

"But what?" I panted. "You choose, my lord." After all, he

had chosen well enough last time, though it had not bought us much time. I thrust out my bag at him as we stumbled along. He took it, plunged his hand down to the bottom, and grasped something.

To my dismay, he held on the palm of his hand the twelve white pebbles. I had told his Highness that our lives were more valuable than any number of rubies. How much more valuable must they be than these common white pebbles? Yet I did not wish to cast them away; I had already lost the feathers and the eggshells. I would now have nothing left of my Geese save the crowns and gowns, which reminded me far more of that wicked old hag than they did of my darling birds.

The Ogresses were upon us. I could hear the harshness of their breathing, smell their graveyard stench. I must throw something.

"Very well." I took the twelve white pebbles in my hand and turning, flung them despairingly right into the Ogresses' faces.

Tessa, Lucinda, and Nellie kept coming.

But yet there was a difference. As the first rays of the sun breasted the peak of the mountain, the Ogresses slowed, stiffened. They moved still toward us, but as though the blood in their veins had congealed, had become some colder, thicker liquid. Their jaws opened, gaped. Their eyes widened; their arms reached toward us in a fury of impotence.

We stood frozen, unable to flee.

A stony scream seemed trying to force itself out of stony throats. Slowly, ponderously, they gathered themselves for one last murderous leap. They leapt; they fell.

They crumbled into great piles of rubble at our feet.

"Goodness!" said the Prince, turning quite pink.

CHAPTER TEN

Little Echo

HASTE IN EVERY BUSINESS BRINGS FAILURES.
—HERODOTUS, *THE HISTORIES OF HERODOTUS*

*T*hey have turned to stone," I whispered. "They are no more."

"They were Ogresses," the Prince said. "Perchance 'twas the sun that turned them to stone and not the pebbles at all."

'Twas true enough that the Ogresses had always returned home ere dawn and left past dark, but yet it had not occurred to me to try to defeat them with daylight.

"I do not know," I said. Then, "It does not matter."

I laid myself down upon the ground just where we stood, next to the piles of crumbled Ogresses. I closed my eyes and slept without dreams for several hours.

"Good morrow, Goose Girl," said the Prince cheerfully when I woke.

I looked about. The sun was high in the sky. The Prince had started a small fire and sat by it looking at his book. I

97

sat up on one elbow and watched him. He was *reading*. I was struck dumb with amazement.

"I have been industrious while you slept," the Prince said virtuously. "I cleared out my saddlebags so as to make them lighter to carry. What a quantity of old roots and bits of plants there was within! I cannot think how they came there; it must have occurred during the fight with the Ogresses."

"You — you what? Old roots, do you say? Bits of plants?"

"Aye. They made the bags quite heavy."

I looked wildly about us. "*What* did you do with them?" I demanded.

"O, I carried them down to that lake we made from eggshells and threw them in. They made a tremendous splash," said Sir Spick-and-Span happily. "Do you know, the lake is still there. I wonder if 'twill always remain, and will the people hereabouts name it after us? That is," he said discontentedly, "if there *are* any people hereabouts. It seems the most dismal wilderness to me."

"You threw them in the lake?" I said in dangerous tones. "All of them?"

"I did," the Prince said, beginning to look a bit wary of me. "Was that not your wish?"

"Considering that Your Highness has flung away our food supplies for a week, no, 'twas not my wish."

"Food? O no, Goose Girl, 'twas not food, but only dead plants and suchlike."

"What, pray tell, does your lordship think that food is, save dead plants and suchlike?"

The Prince looked crushed. "Ah. I see. I am deeply grieved. I—I did not think. I have contributed many a bird to the pot at home, but I am ignorant of cookery else."

"In certes, sire, I hope that you will contribute a bird or two to *our* pot, else we shall starve," I said grimly.

The Prince had turned pale and sat silent staring for a time at the fire. "I perceive that I am naught but a burden to you, Goose Girl," he said at length. "In the cottage of the Ogresses I unwittingly betrayed you in the matter of the scissors, and now I have destroyed provisions carefully gathered by you for our flight. I am most humbly sorry."

And indeed, he seemed to be so. There glimmered a tear in his eye and I remembered that he was little older than I was myself. I felt much like weeping as well. I could, of course, find a few of those plants as we traveled, but this was different country here in the hills than below us in the Ogresses' valley; 'twas drier, with great towering trees and little underbrush.

The Prince stood up. He replaced his book within the saddlebags and withdrew his bow and his arrows, those that were left from the encounter with the Ogresses.

"I am generally accounted a good shot," he said. "I would have gone in search of game while you slept, did I not fear to alarm you by my absence when you woke. I will not fail you now."

He looked up at the sky, fitting an arrow to his bow.
A bird was flying overhead. 'Twas white as snow, and fair.
Swift as thought he drew the bow tight.
"No!" I shrieked. "No!"
The bow twanged and an arrow sped forward, heedless.
Silence. Then a cry that would haunt my dreams.
Little Echo tumbled to our feet, an arrow in her chest.

"Murderer! Go thou hence and leave me!" I sobbed, hunched over Little Echo's poor white corpse.

"I am sorry, Goose Girl, but how was I to know 'twas one of *your* Geese?" asked the Prince, looking nervously about himself at the other eleven Geese, who were landed, and now formed a menacing circle about him. "I have *said* I was sorry more times than I can count. What else would you have me do?"

"Leave me," I repeated curtly.

One of the Geese—I think 'twas Lydia-the-Loud— nipped at his foot. Stealthily he aimed a kick in her direction, but desisted when he saw that I was watching.

"Go," I said, and pointed toward the direction we had come. "Go away."

"Nay, I will not," he said, shaking his head.

"Sire, you promised to do my bidding. I bid you go."

"I will not. Stand back, birds," he said, waving his arms at the Geese in an aggressive manner.

"What of your honor? What of your word?"

"O, aye, I know, but 'tis complicated, Goose Girl."

"'Tis most assuredly *not*! I bid you go. Now go!"

He shook his head decisively. "I have done you wrong, Goose Girl, not once but thrice. Three times have I harmed you, though I never meant to. I cannot now leave you without making amends."

"*Four* times," I corrected him.

"Nay," he said, puzzled. "'Twas but three." He knitted his brows and counted on his fingers. "One: that I did let the Ogress know you possessed the scissors. Two: that I did lay waste our food supply. Three: that I did kill your most dearly beloved Goose."

"The tower, Prince. Pray do not forget six months' detention in the tower."

"But that was for your protection! Were you not well treated?"

"O, well treated! Aye, Your Majesty, I was well treated save for the fact, the small, insignificant fact, that I was robbed of my liberty."

The Prince grew red in the face. "Would you rather have lost your liberty in the King's dungeons, there to languish until your death? Your life has been a sheltered one in the forest, Goose Girl, so perhaps it is not surprising that you know little of men. I must tell you that the King"—he lowered his voice and whispered in my ear for fear of eavesdroppers in this vast unpeopled wasteland—"is not a nice man." He shook his head. "No indeed, Goose Girl, not a nice man at all. I may say no more to one of your sex and lack of experience."

Nearly choking with rage, I cried, "Then why did you not bar him from your country? Why do you allow him to bring soldiers upon your lands to menace your subjects?"

"Because his army is larger than mine," said the Prince simply.

I was silent, having no ready response. Eugenia butted me with her head, wanting attention, but I pushed her away.

"Marriage to me," the Prince said, "was the greatest, indeed the only, security you could have. If you did not choose it, why then, you were best off in the tower, where the King would have to declare open warfare and bring a great force of men in order to capture you.

"And, do you know," he went on, sounding a bit hurt, "I thought that you might be quite pleased to marry me. My councillors tell me that my hand is greatly sought after both at home and abroad. I was much criticized, in fact, for offering to marry you, though you brought so much wealth. I might have married the Princess Chlotilde of Broome and thereby united our countries. Instead I chose to marry a Goose Girl who was coveted by the King of Gilboa, which put my life, and the welfare of our country, at risk."

So the Prince had realized how dangerous our marriage would have been to him. And yet . . .

"Do you mean to say that my gold and diamonds had naught to do with your courtship?"

"O well," he said, blushing, "perhaps a trifle."

He grew gloomy. "Now for certain sure they are most tremendously wroth because I would go in search of you. If

I die, Old Pennyfavor—he is chief of all my father's councillors, and the fussiest old fudgeon you ever did meet—Pennyfavor will be *so* annoyed if I die. I am the only child of my father, who, as you may know, is failing in health."

Since I had been born a subject of the Prince's, I quite naturally did know. "Humph," was all I could find to say in reply. Penelope nibbled at my fingers and honked dolefully, but I ignored her.

"So far as my other misdeeds are concerned, I have nothing to urge in excuse, save ignorance. Indeed, I am sorry about your Goose, Little— What did you call her?"

"Little Echo," I muttered sullenly.

"Well do I understand your feelings, having recently lost a most tenderly loved horse under particularly horrible circumstances."

I flushed uncomfortably and began, "Your Highness, that stew was not—" when Simple Sophia bit my arm.

"Stop it at once, Simple Sophia!" I cried, abandoning my explanations to chastise my Goose.

"Nay, Goose Girl, but I think—indeed I am certain, that your good Geese in their wisdom are trying to tell you something." He smiled and pointed at the body of Little Echo.

I whirled about, furious. What, pray tell, could the Prince find so amusing in that pathetic sight?

"See? She stirs. She is not dead at all."

I cried out and dropped to my knees beside her.

"Soft! Have a care, Goose Girl. She may not be dead but she is surely sore wounded."

The Prince had removed the arrow in the first dreadful moments after she fell. The bleeding had stopped, and so I had assumed that she was no more.

"O my poor Little Echo! She was wounded less than a fortnight ago, in much the same place. 'Tis a great wonder she did not die."

"The wonder is that I did not hit her square. I would not wish you to gain a poor idea of my skills as a marksman. You must have joggled my arm as I released the arrow, Goose Girl."

I regarded him coldly. "So I must hope, my lord." I returned to consideration of Little Echo's needs.

'Twas difficult to continue being out of charity with the Prince, however. He was so pleased at Little Echo's having rejoined the living, so genuinely helpful in fetching water to be heated over the fire and rigging up a comfortable bed inside the saddlebags in order to carry her with us when we left in the morning, that I had not the heart to dislike him further.

I wanted to carry Little Echo myself, naturally, but now that the Prince had got rid of our food, there was far more room in the saddlebags than in my sewing kit.

We were headed home, to Dorloo. I knew not where else in the world to go. The cottage of the Ogresses, where once I had thought to live, was now inaccessible behind a mountain of snow and a great lake. I had the Prince's word, for what it was worth, that he would defend my right to remain a single woman. Perchance I might find some other cottage in his realm, far from the border to Gilboa, where I could live in strict retirement and thus escape the King's notice.

And so in the morning the Prince cheerfully shouldered the saddlebags and walked off down the ridge with nary a sigh or moan over Little Echo's weight, which was not inconsiderable. I walked beside him and the other Geese waddled placidly ahead of us. Our stomachs were not quite empty, for I had found a good quantity of acorns which I roasted over the fire and a handful of berries to sweeten our repast. The Prince had grumbled a bit over the coarse and scanty nature of the meal, but catching my eye, he fell silent.

As we walked along I asked him, "Why, Your Highness, did you follow me, and why did not the King? And how did you manage it? We flew, my Geese and I, and left no trail. How did you track us through air?"

The Prince opened his mouth and then closed it. I had confused him with too many questions. I rephrased my inquiry.

"I pray you, my lord, tell me what happened after I escaped from the tower."

The expression on the Prince's face cleared at once. "We were much amazed," he began, "when we perceived the featherbeds rising from the tower. We had no thought of you being upon them, as we believed you to be within your chambers. You were *supposed* to remain within your chambers." He frowned at my willful ways. "Although," he added, "now that I think on it, you might have grown a bit dull, always remaining within those few apartments. In truth, 'twould have been enough to drive me mad. Was it dull for you, Goose Girl?"

"It was, sire."

"I gave you a little bird from the Canary Islands, thinking that it would cheer you; what happened to it?"

"The King killed it, sire."

"Ah! I am sorry for that. Well then, when once I found that you were gone, I followed you, only pausing to demand a goodly store of provisions from the cook ere setting out to rescue you. I am of an impetuous nature," he said, smiling in a self-satisfied manner. "Also, had I returned home, they would not have let me go."

"And the King, sire? What did he say when he knew I was gone?"

The Prince looked discomfited. "I may not say."

"Sire?"

"His — his language," he said, obviously much embarrassed, "'tis not fit for a maiden's ears."

"I see. And after he cursed me roundly, then what did he do?"

"He went home."

"Home?" I said, my hopes rising. "Do you mean that he has renounced all claims to my hand?" Perhaps, just perhaps, I might go to my own home again and live in peace.

"As to that I could not say. What he said was that he had other fish to fry, at present."

I pondered. "What," I wondered aloud, "could he mean by that?"

"I do not of course know, but 'twas my belief that he meant the peasant rebellion. I thought mayhap that would be occupying his time and attention for the immediate future."

"Which peasant rebellion, my lord?" I asked patiently.

"Why the King of Gilboa's peasant rebellion, of course. Really, Goose Girl, I had not thought you such a clumperton. Who else have we been discussing?"

"Do you mean to tell me that those poor, oppressed people have risen up against the King after all?"

"They have. Do you know, I rather think it may be unwise for a ruler to spend a *great* deal of time away from home, especially if he is not much loved by the populace. The populace may get the idea into its head that 'twould be possible to muddle along without him. Which idea may be decidedly dangerous for the ruler, you see.

"For the past six months the King has been courting you, Goose Girl, and I don't believe he is widely admired by his subjects. I know that *I* never much cared for him. He is an usurper, you know. He is not the rightful King."

"Is that so, my lord?" I asked absently, not much interested in the doings of the King of Gilboa, so long as he remained far distant. "But now tell me, Prince—"

"I, of course, am much beloved by my people. *Much* beloved."

"O, in certes, sire."

"One might almost say I am adored."

"No doubt. But —"

"You ought to have seen that cook, Goose Girl. She couldn't show me enough attention. 'Twas almost embarrassing."

"I have no difficulty imagining it, my lord," I sighed. "Indeed, your subjects love you well."

"*You* are one of my subjects, Goose Girl." The Prince looked slyly at me out of the corner of his eye. "Dost thou love thy prince and lord?"

"Of a surety, sire," I said, not at all caring for the trend of this conversation. "As your subject, of course. We have settled to our own satisfaction that no other relationship between us is possible."

"Hmmm . . . true," said the Prince, and he was silent.

"But you have not told me, sire," I said, "how 'twas that you found me. You came upon the Ogresses' valley in less than a fortnight, and I cannot think how you managed it."

"O, that was the easiest thing in the world," the Prince said negligently. "I take no credit for it."

"But how was it *done*?" I demanded, grinding my teeth only a little.

"Why, your Geese showed me the way, of course, how else?"

"My — my Geese? What can you mean?"

Patiently, as though speaking to a child, the Prince said, "Your Geese led me to you, I tell you. They found me in a lonely wood, quite despairing. Some walked before me and some walked after, never allowing me to stray from the path which they had ordained." The Prince rubbed his hindmost portions reminiscently. "They can be quite severe when they choose to be, your Geese."

CHAPTER ELEVEN

In Which We Are Arrested

CHILDREN AND FOOLS CANNOT LIE.
— JOHN HEYWOOD, PROVERBS

"Sssso!" I hissed at Ernestina the moment I could do so without drawing the Prince's attention. "This is how you protect me and keep me from want, as my mother promised. You saddle me with worthless Princes. What! Did you think that I needed the Prince's help to escape from the Ogresses?"

Actually, 'twas true that the Prince *had* been rather helpful in some ways, but did my Geese really imagine that I could not have managed to get free without his aid?

Ernestina rolled her eyes. Enraged, I pinched her. Alberta waddled over, protesting. I pinched her too. The Geese all became agitated and milled about, hissing and shaking their bills.

"Hunh, hunh hunh!" they cried in indignation.

"Er," said the Prince diffidently, "I am sorry to interrupt your consultation with your friends, Goose Girl, but there seems to be a rather large group of soldiers approaching us through the trees."

"What? O Hades!"

The Geese immediately all launched themselves into the air in a body, passing low over the soldiers' heads and distracting them while the Prince and I fled.

I heard the soldiers shooting at my gallant Geese and could not help turning around to watch anxiously as we ran. The Prince at length grasped my hand in his and pulled me along.

The soldiers, I was pleased to see, were inexperienced in handling their muskets. I was a better shot than any of them. The soldiers' technique seemed to be to point, shoot, and then immediately fall over backwards onto the ground. This did not improve their aim. As all of them tried in turn to bring down a Goose, their company rather gave the impression of a great number of jack-in-the-boxes popping up and down between the trees. To the best of my observation, not one of my Geese was hit.

Their bravery was all for naught. One soldier, more alert than his fellows, espied us running away and alarmed the others.

"We must climb a tree," gasped the Prince. "'Tis our only hope."

'Twas not much of a hope. My Princess gown, though torn in scrambling out of the tower and partly ripped up for bandages, still retained its rich coloring, and my cursed hair shone bright as a whole treasure house of gold. The Prince's white satin tunic was soiled and spotted with dirt and grass stains, but yet gleamed moony white in the shadow of the trees.

The Prince chose a mighty oak with a convenient low-hanging branch. He scrambled up right smartly.

I whispered, "O, do be careful of Little Echo!"

He nodded, reached out an arm, and dragged me up after him. I will own that I appreciated his help. A Princess gown is not the best attire for climbing trees.

Once ensconced in the tree, we sat in silence and watched the soldiers running toward us. A thought struck me.

"Do not the uniforms of those soldiers look very much like those of the King of Gilboa's?" I whispered.

"That is because they are the King of Gilboa's soldiers," explained the Prince.

"But that cannot be! We must be many miles away from Gilboa."

"Nay, Goose Girl. You have never left Gilboa since you departed the tower and flew over the border."

"But—!"

The Prince silenced me by placing his forefinger on my lips. The soldiers had drawn very near. 'Twas evident by their behavior that they knew we were close by and were searching for us amongst the trees.

Biting my lips as I watched them, I reflected that I would never have guessed that Gilboa was so very large a country. 'Twas sad, really, to think that so much land should be under the rule of a man like the King.

They did not find us at once, and for a time I hoped they would not at all. Indeed I began to think that unless we set the tree afire they would never notice us in it. Twice the Prince sneezed while a soldier stood below, and once a foraging squirrel discerned us and set to scolding us for invading a favorite nutting tree.

I blush to say that 'twas an act of mine that brought discovery down on us. Something—I cannot say what, but some small insect—bit my leg quite painfully and it twitched uncontrollably. Off flew my little glass slipper and struck a soldier violently on the head. He caught it as it rebounded and regarded it quizzically.

"'Od's bodkin!" he muttered, scratching his pate. "Shoes from the sky. Now there's a wonder for you! Pretty little thing, too, all made o' glass. I expect," he said, his eyes widening as the explanation came to him, "it belongs to an angel. She'd be flyin' by, ye see," he explained to a nonexistent companion, "an' givin' a little flirt o' her wings and a kick o' her heels, it mighta fallen off, accidental-like." He rubbed his hand over his mouth, and his face lit up with sudden cunning. "I wonder now," he asked his invisible friend, "just how much money do ye reckon a thing like this might bring in at the market fair in Clove City? A gen-yoo-wine certified angel shoe like this here one?" He answered himself with considerable satisfaction, "A pretty penny, that's what. A pretty penny."

I reached out a hand and gripped the Prince's in mine, holding my breath. Could it be that even now, after the

113

disaster of the slipper, we should be saved? The soldier, overcome with greed, was about to hide the "angel's" shoe in his tunic, when his superior officer appeared and spotted it.

"What, pray, is that, Smeatt?"

"O nowt, nowt at all, sir."

"Where, Smeatt, did you get that woman's shoe?"

"'Tis not a woman's shoe, sir, but footgear belonging to a member of the Heavenly Host, and not for your delectation, sir, nor mine."

"Give me that shoe, Smeatt."

"O, sir!"

"How came you by this shoe, Smeatt?" demanded the officer, taking my slipper in his hand.

"It fell from the sky, sir, it did. From the heel of an angel, sir. 'Tis holy, like."

The officer looked up into the tree at us.

"There is your angel, Smeatt."

Smeatt looked up and his jaw dropped.

"Why, so she is, sir. And I'm sure I'll be a better man from now on, knowing what it is I have to look forward to, iffen I behave meself in this world."

"Yes, well, while we are awaiting that event, why don't you help the lady down out of the tree, and the gentleman as well?" And the officer aimed his musket at the Prince's heart.

Given this troop of soldiers' known lack of ability with gunpowder, you might think we were fools to come down, but we were sitting targets, and where, after all, was there for us to go?

We came down.

"Identify yourselves," demanded the officer crisply.

"O sir," I said, endeavoring to look helpless and innocent and devastatingly beautiful, all at once, "we are but poor Gooseherders, whose flock has gone astray. Mayhap you saw them, as you were coming through the wood?"

The Prince jabbed me with his elbow. I jabbed him right back. Had he any other ideas? Finding the King's missing bride as well as the King's rival for her hand, wandering far from home on the King's own land, would be a prodigious feather in this man's cap.

"We saw them," said the officer, but he did not offer to let us go after pointing out the direction they had taken. Instead he turned to Smeatt, who had been fluttering his eyelashes soulfully in my direction.

"Arrest them," he said briefly, and turned away.

"Sir!" Smeatt cried out as though he had been struck. "O my Gawd, sir!" he pleaded. "Say y'don't mean it, sir!"

"I do mean it, Smeatt. If that young woman is a Goose Girl, why then I am the Empress of China."

Smeatt appeared nearly overcome at this wholly unexpected possibility.

"O sir!"

"She is no more a Goose Girl than she is an angel. And even supposing her to be telling the truth, then how did she come by that crown she is wearing? And this glass slipper? And the gown she wears, tattered though it is? The only possible answer is: dishonestly."

Smeatt appeared to be struck by this reasoning. "That crown, sir. I do believe . . ."

"Believe what, man? Speak up."

Smeatt shook his head. "Nowt, sir. I said nowt concerning the crown."

The officer examined him for a moment, but as Smeatt assumed a particularly wooden expression, he went on.

"And as for the man," he said, warming to his theme, "come now, Smeatt. Do you think that men tend geese while all tricked out in white satin and metal breastplates? Who they are I cannot say, but who they say they are is assuredly not who they are."

Smeatt's eyes nearly popped out of his head with the difficulty of following this.

His commanding officer eyed him severely. "I shall send you some reinforcements to make certain you have every assistance you require."

"But — but what shall I do with 'em, sir?" asked Smeatt piteously.

"Escort the noble fowl tenders to the castle of the Baroness of Breakabeen. I am sure her ladyship would be pleased to entertain them until the King has leisure to inspect them."

My heart sank clear down to the ground.

The Prince cleared his throat.

"How goes the peasant revolt?" he asked. My heart rebounded suddenly. I had forgot the peasant revolt entirely. Mayhap things were not so bad after all.

The officer's eyebrows shot up.

"What do you say? Peasant revolt? What peasant revolt?"

"The peasant revolt here in Gilboa. Why, I heard it from—" The Prince checked himself. "That is, I pray your mercy, sir. 'Tis obvious I am in error."

"From whom did you receive this information?" demanded the officer sharply.

"O, from nobody in particular," said the Prince feebly. "'Twas only in the air, so to speak."

"I see, Sir Swineherd, or whatever you call yourself. 'Tis clear to me that I have caught myself a very pretty pair indeed. There is no peasant revolt in Gilboa, no, nor any other sort of revolt. Our King has little patience with that sort of thing. He will be most interested to hear what you have to say, no doubt." He handed me my slipper, bowed very low, and walked away.

I closed my eyes. 'Twould not be the tower this time, with little caged singing birds and golden goblets, but rather the King's dungeons for me, and perchance the scaffold for the Prince. I swayed a little as I stood, and the Prince gripped my arm to prevent me from falling.

"Excuse me, miss," said Smeatt. I opened my eyes and saw him standing there with a bit of twine in his hands. "I mean Yer Holiness, that is. Begging your pardon, but I got to tie yer hands together. I know it's a dretful liberty and I'm

117

most humbly sorry, but I got to do what the Major tells me to do, ye see, or I'm finished. 'Tis a hard life in this here army and that's the truth."

I looked wildly around. I saw the Prince do the same. There were two of us to one of him, and that one a fool. Of course, one of our number was a fool as well, but still — a wild dash for the forest and then . . .

Five more soldiers appeared, aiming their muskets at us.

"Tell me that you will forgive me, ma'am," begged Smeatt.

"I forgive you, Smeatt," I said sadly, and held out my wrists.

"By all the saints!" gasped Smeatt in terror. "What did I tell ye?" He appealed to his invisible companion. "Now how did she know my name?"

"O, Smeatt," I sighed. Verily, my Prince was beginning to take on the appearance of a wise and rational human being in comparison with this Smeatt.

When once we were tied to Smeatt's satisfaction, we began walking, surrounded by soldiers.

"I do not understand it," muttered the Prince under his breath. "Why would the King have told me there was a peasants' revolt if there was nothing of the sort?"

"Perchance the officer is in ignorance of it?" I suggested, though in the event of a revolt, surely the army would be the first to be informed.

"Smeatt!" the Prince said loudly.

Smeatt made a gesture to avert the evil eye. "Him too!" he wailed. "That one knows my name too!"

"Smeatt," said the Prince, "what was this troop of men doing when you found us? Where were you going?"

Smeatt rolled his eyes like a startled horse and then looked hopefully around at his fellow soldiers for guidance. They all avoided his gaze and began looking up into the sky, or whistling a tune, or examining the cut of their fingernails.

"O sir, I can't tell yer that. Indeed, I can't. I'd get into 'orrible, 'orrible trouble iffen I did that."

"And why is that, pray tell, Smeatt?" the Prince demanded, lifting an eyebrow in inquiry, his voice as authoritative as a lifetime of giving orders could make it.

Smeatt looked desperately at the other soldiers, but they went on disassociating themselves as much as possible from this little drama.

"Well, Smeatt? Why may you not tell me what I ask?"

"O, because it might get around to the Prince of Dorloo, that's why, sir."

"And why would that be a problem, Smeatt?" said the Prince in a terrible voice.

"O, sir, because."

"Because *why*?"

"Because we be takin' over his country while he's off chasin' after some girl," finished Smeatt in a rush. "That's why, sir."

CHAPTER TWELVE

The Bad Baroness
of Breakabeen

THE MOON IS MADE OF A GREEN CHEESE.
— JOHN HEYWOOD, PROVERBS

*B*y my troth, I really fail to comprehend why I should
feel the slightest pang of guilt that the King of Gilboa has
chosen to invade Dorloo. In what way was it my fault, pray?
Had I put the idea into the King's head? Had I asked the
Prince to come chasing off after me into the wilds of Gilboa?
No indeed, I had not.

Nonetheless, I found it difficult to meet the Prince's eye
after this blow had been delivered. Innocent though I be, I
was yet the reason why my own country might fall into the
hands of that dreadful and bloodthirsty tyrant, the King, as
well as being the likely instrument of the Prince's death.

After we had stumbled along in silence for a time, I muttered in a barely audible voice, "I—I am more grieved than
I can say, s—" I stopped myself just in time before I said
"sire."

The Prince looked up, his eyes dazed with horror. "My

father—he is ill and wandering in his wits. I do not know what to do, Goose Girl. There is no one to defend the country, no one to lead—" His eyes flicked around at the soldiers on each side, and I saw him realize the inadvisability of revealing our identities. 'Twould not be for long, but yet we must do all we could to delay their learning who we were.

The Prince straightened his spine and looked straight ahead. "'Tis best we do not speak of it."

"Aye," I agreed. "'Tis best." We walked henceforward in silence.

Soon the donjon of a castle showed above the trees and a turn in the path revealed the whole. I noticed with apprehension that this was no civilized palace, but an armed fortress on the banks of a wide river. Steep-sided walls, unrelieved by any windows save a line of mean-looking arrow slits, reared up over us, and a great iron portcullis slammed down behind us with a tremendous crash when once we were admitted to the premises. No doubt, being located in this wilderness, 'twas necessary to be ready for trouble, but 'twas not in any way a welcoming place to visitors such as ourselves.

The Major had joined us, no doubt in order to take credit for our capture, though he had as yet no idea what a prize he had to offer. He walked at the head of our procession, looking well content with himself.

The Great Hall of the Baroness's citadel was a bleak enough place. I found myself looking about rather critically as we were marched through the enormous, drafty place. 'Twas like a great black cave. There was little light and less furniture or decoration. No tapestries or hangings softened the stark stone walls. A mob of rats scampered away, squealing mightily, as we approached over the greasy, filth-bestrewn floor rushes. The lady of the house was evidently unworried by a trifling degree of dirt and disorder.

The Baroness was to be found, not in her Great Hall, but in a small room behind it, which was furnished with a chair, a table, and a bench with a broken leg. She sat at the table, writing.

As we entered she looked up briefly.

"Sit," she barked, gesturing at the bench with the broken leg.

Since our party was too numerous to fit on the bench, the Major sent his six soldiers outside to guard the door, while he himself chose to stand. We two were left eyeing the broken bench dubiously.

I caught the Prince's eye. "Both together," I suggested, and smiled cheerfully at him, an "Is-not-this-an-adventure?" sort of smile. For some reason, I did not think I could bear to see him looking so tragic.

The Prince nodded gloomily and we simultaneously lowered our backsides onto the bench.

The Baroness went on, scribbling on a large piece of parchment. For a while there was silence while she wrote and we examined her. She was built on similar lines to her castle, large-boned and solid. She looked as though her only recreation was crushing boulders with her bare hands. She sported a small, black mustache on her upper lip and thick, heavy black braids wound round and round her head.

"How do you spell 'massacre'?" she demanded suddenly.

The Major appeared to feel that this query was directed at us and not at him. He smiled vacantly and studied the ceiling.

"You there. The yellow-haired girl. How do you you spell 'massacre'?"

"I regret to say that I cannot be of service to you, Madam Baroness."

"Can't read, eh?"

"That is correct, Your Ladyship," I said, flushing with annoyance.

"And you, boy? Do you know?"

"Certainly, madam." The Prince sprang to his feet and bowed deeply, incidentally precipitating me onto the floor in a heap as the bench overbalanced.

When once I had been picked up, dusted off, apologized to, and replaced on the bench, the Prince cautiously reseated himself as well and said precisely, "The correct spelling of 'massacre' is m-a-s-s-a-c-r-e, madam."

"Hmmm . . . as you know so much, tell me then: should I write 'hanged' or 'hung'?"

"That, madam, would depend on whether you wish to hang men or pictures."

"O, let it be men, by all means. Or"— she glanced slyly at me — "maids, if you prefer."

"No, indeed," he said, turning rather paler. "One says that a man is hanged and a picture is hung."

"It is of little significance," she said, nevertheless altering her manuscript. "I don't suppose the King of Gilboa cares one way or another." She looked up suddenly and fixed him with her eye. "What is your opinion?"

I held my breath.

"I could not say," said the Prince coldly, and I breathed again. The Prince could not be trusted to lie, but at least he had not fallen into the trap and admitted to knowing the King.

She signed her name and title with a great slashing flourish, folded the document, and was about to close it up with sealing wax when she paused.

"Nay, I suppose I had best leave this open until I fathom what you pair are about, wandering through my demesne pretending to be overdressed, overeducated cowherds."

"Geese, not cows," I could not help interrupting.

"Geese," she said, shooting me a look in which there was little friendliness. "And so, Goldilocks, you claim to be a humble Goose Girl, do you, taking the air with your learned colleague here, the Goose Boy?"

I gave the Prince a meaningful look to warn him both to agree with the story I was about to tell and also that I meant to stand up. The bench rocked dangerously as I rose, but did not quite overturn.

"Your Ladyship," I said and curtsied so low I felt my knee bones crack. "'Tis true enough that I am a Goose Girl, but my companion is not, as you in your wisdom have seen. Nay, my sweetheart and I"—here I sensed rather than saw the Prince start so violently that he nearly capsized the bench—"are instead privileged citizens of the Golden Isles, that happy, blessed land on the western rim of the world, where the rivers run with wine, rubies and emeralds grow on golden trees, and the pigs fly about on silvery wings all day, singing like larks in a meadow."

The Baroness's eyes narrowed upon hearing this last piece of invention. I went on quickly.

"Judging by our dress you think that we are of noble birth. We are not. *All* the inhabitants of the Golden Isles dress in satins and velvets and golden crowns. He is but a lowly tutor to the Princess Gloribelle Graciella while I am her Goose Girl."

"O, aye? And what, prithee, are you doing on my lands? It cannot have escaped your notice that you are no longer in the Golden Isles."

"No, Your Ladyship." I curtsied again. "We are run away from our homes in order to wed. My dearest"—and here I searched my mind frantically for a man's name—"Osbert," I continued triumphantly, "has been expressly forbidden by his parents to wed me as I am but a poor orphan. Without parental permission we should never have been allowed to join our fates. So we have run far, far away in hopes of finding someone to marry us, after which we plan to return home and present his parents with an established fact."

The Baroness studied us in silence for a moment.

"I do believe," she said at last, "that that is the veriest load of hogslop I have ever heard in the whole compass of my days."

Now was the moment for me to give my best performance. I had never thought that the Baroness would believe my first tale: she was not the sort. I sank to my knees and pressed my forehead to the stone floor, my bound wrists extended before me.

"'Tis true! I swear it!"

When the Baroness continued to look skeptically at me, I cried out in terror—'twas not difficult for me to pretend to this emotion.

"O my lady, I do beseech you! 'Tis true, or at least, 'tis nearly all true."

"Oho, now we are coming to it. Do you wish to retract the flying pigs, perchance?"

"Yes, yes. I ought not to have tried to fool a woman of your sagacity, I see that now.

"'Tis true enough that my Osbert is a tutor and I a Goose Girl, but we hail from the court of the Princess Chlotilde of Broome, not from the Golden Isles, if Golden Isles there be. We did indeed wish to wed but were forbidden, for his parents think him far too good for me. As indeed he is." I bowed my head remorsefully and nearly squeezed out a tear until I remembered that 'twould be a diamond, which was the last item required in the circumstances.

"We made a scheme, as I told, to steal away to be wed in

another country, and I—I am deeply ashamed to admit—"
I dropped my head into my hands and groaned aloud.

"Well, get on with it. What did you do?"

"Without Osbert's knowledge I took—I abstracted—"

"O, a thief, is it?" asked the Baroness with an ironic smile.

"Aye, 'tis true enough. These things"—I gestured at my
crown and my dress — "belong to the Princess Chlotilde.
Osbert's suit of clothes belongs to the King, her father. 'Twas
none of Osbert's doing, lady. He had no guilty knowledge,
even. I told him the things belonged to my aunt, now dead.
He is a good man, my Bertie, but not overly sharp in his
wits. Clever enough at his books," I admitted handsomely,
"but unworldly. I beg you, let him go to make his way
home, a sadder but wiser man."

The Prince leapt to his feet with a clatter as the bench
overturned once again. "'Tis a lie!" he roared. "Every word is
false. I swear upon my honor as Prince Edmund Percival
Augustus Bernardus Blenheim, Crown Prince of Dorloo, that
there is not an atom of truth to the Goose Girl's statement."

The Baroness shifted in her chair to regard him with interest.

"Nay!" I cried. "I pray you, do not listen. Osbert is—he
is wandering in his mind. We suffered greatly, wandering in
the forest, and he is half mad from want. We have supped
on naught but a handful of acorns and berries this day," I
said quite truthfully and turned to glare threateningly at His
Highness.

"She lies," the Prince said, quite calm now. He folded his arms over his chest and took up an aggressive stance before the Baroness. "Most nobly, but she lies."

The Baroness spoke. "Whether *she* lies or *he* lies, 'tis clear enough that I may let neither of you go at present. I am sure that you understand that well enough, Goose Girl." She smiled sardonically at me. "You are an intelligent child."

I bowed my head. There had only been a very small chance of freeing the Prince, in any case. Still, he need not have made the Baroness a present of every name he possessed, need he?

The Baroness's gaze suddenly sharpened.

"A Goose Girl in the company of the Prince of Dorloo!" She stared at me, and her eyes grew hard as little pebbles. "So! Perhaps you might be the Goose Girl in whom my fiancé has been expressing such an interest, this past half year."

"Your fiancé?" I said, puzzled by the introduction of this new character.

"Aye. Mayhap you were unaware that the King of Gilboa is my most dearly beloved affianced husband. Since earliest childhood."

"Indeed?" I said feebly. "How — how charming. I do congratulate you both."

The Prince looked confused. "But Goose Girl, I thought that the King of Gilboa wanted to marry —"

"I cannot say how pleased I am to hear it," I said, very loudly. "He seems to need a wife, somehow, and I am sure you will fill the role to a perfection." My foot sought the Prince's booted one and pressed it. He opened his mouth to protest.

"Goose Girl," he complained, but then seemed to understand and remained silent.

"You call her 'Goose Girl,'" said the Baroness, a bitter smile playing on her lips, "yet if gossip speaks true, you wished to marry the young woman. I understand she possesses certain . . . talents, besides her pretty face." She looked at me in silence for a moment, eyeing my golden curls and perfect profile with obvious distaste, then turned back to the Prince. "What is her name? Or do you not know it? It may not have mattered to you, but I always like to know the names of my guests. We know yours in full; what is hers?"

The Prince turned red as fire. "I — I do not know," he admitted. "I have always called her 'Goose Girl.' Or 'my lady,' back when — " He looked wretched. Back when he was still attempting to woo me, is what he had been about to say.

"Well? Your name?" the Baroness inquired of me.

"Alexandria Aurora Fortunato, madam," I said, and curtsied.

The crooked smile that the Baroness had worn slipped and faded. The muscles of her face went slack. She half rose from her chair, her hands gripped into fists on the table.

"What!"

Much amazed, I repeated, "Alexandria Aurora Fortunato, Your Ladyship."

"No!" she murmured to herself, sinking back into her seat. "It cannot be. They were all killed. *All* of them."

She stared at me intensely, her eyes expressionless black pools. At length she ordered, "Look over there!" and pointed at the wall to my left.

Startled, I looked, but there was naught to see. 'Twas but a blank stone wall. I returned my gaze to hers.

"Mayhap. It might be so," she muttered. "There is a resemblance. And that crown. I have seen that before as well." Then, abruptly, "Does *he* know?"

"Your Ladyship?" I inquired, all at sea.

"*Does he know?*" she roared.

"He whom?" I asked desperately.

"The King of Gilboa, thou gongoozling grinagog! Who didst thou think I meant?"

"And — and what does Your Honor wish to know if he knows?" I said, fearing to provoke her to a fit of greater violence.

"Thy name, thou golden-haired ninny! Thy name!"

"Why, no. I don't suppose he did. He certainly never called me by it, or inquired it of me. Did he know my name, do you think, sire?" I asked the Prince.

The Prince looked as much befogged as I. "Nay, I do not know, Goose Girl — that is, Mistress Alexandria, if so I may call you. And on this topic, I must tender you my very abject apologies. You see, given the fact that our stations in life are so different —"

"Never mind that," the Baroness snarled. "Did you ever hear him speak her name?"

"Nay, I did not."

The Baroness fell silent. Then slowly, she smiled. Her smile was not for us, but entirely in response to her own thoughts. I felt a chill wash through my whole body though I did not know why.

She stood up and walked to the door.

"You there," she called to the soldiers. "Get in here."

They came, looking to the Major for guidance.

"Perform whatsoever this lady commands," he instructed them. The Major appeared to be unsettled by the Baroness's manner and unwilling to cross her.

She pointed at the Prince and me.

"Seize them and bind them," she said. "Throw them into the dungeons." Out of the room she stalked, her whole person taut with determination.

CHAPTER THIRTEEN

Down in the Dungeon

NOTHING IS IMPOSSIBLE
TO A WILLING HEART.
— JOHN HEYWOOD, PROVERBS

At once, an argument broke out among the soldiers about how best to do the lady's bidding. The Major had departed in pursuit of the Baroness, probably hoping to receive some refreshment and thanks for his part in our capture, so that we were alone with the soliders.

"Bind 'em, she sez," said one soldier gloomily. "But they be already bound." He gestured toward our bound wrists.

"Tie their ankles, too," suggested another soldier.

"But then we'd have to carry 'em, and we don't even know where these precious dungeons is."

"Untie us," I proposed, "and then *retie* us."

"O, no, y'don't, lady," said the first soldier. "We don't be so stupid as we look, not by an ell, we don't."

Privately reserving my opinion on this, I held my tongue.

"The long and the short of it," he went on, "is that we don't got anything to bind 'em *with*. And Smeatt here, he be

132

the one that bound 'em, so you could say we already done that, couldn't you?"

The other soldiers nodded solemnly. Smeatt made a complicated face at me which apparently was intended to convey apology.

"Well, now. Then the next thing to do is to figure out where these dungeons be an' toss 'em down 'em. You there, Smeatt, didn't you used to be in this here Baroness's service?"

More apologetic wrigglings and grimaces from Smeatt.

"Now then, y'little scobberlotcher," said the soldier, grasping Smeatt by the nape of his neck and shaking him violently, "stop all that squirmin' an' speak up. D'you know where they be?"

"I — er, I do, mates. Beg pardon, miss," he said, grinning nervously at me.

"That's right," said the first soldier, "you just show us."

I had hoped that the Prince and I might be flung into the same dungeon, but alas! we were separated. Considering that this was the castle of a mere Barony, I thought it rather ostentatious to possess more than one dungeon, but presumably the Barons of Breakabeen were a quarrelsome breed who thought themselves ill-equipped without half a score of these gloomy apartments.

"Here be one, fer the lady," said Smeatt, when we had traveled down to the ground floor of the castle. He lifted a trapdoor in the floor which emptied into a chamber carved out of the great rock on which the castle was built. "It be the State Dungeon, like, fer Very Important Prisoners. 'Tis the best there is on offer, lady," he said apologetically. "The others all be full to the brim with bats and suchlike vermin. You wouldn't like them."

"That's enough o' that," said the first soldier. "Now you just pick 'er up and toss 'er down."

I flinched, for the stone floor was twenty feet below.

"I'll not trouble you," I said. I set my feet on the top rungs of the rope ladder and began climbing down.

"Aye, what do be the matter of ye, Baldroon?" demanded Smeatt of his colleague. "That's a lady, that is, if she don't be somethin' higher an' greater. Y'can see it writ all over 'er lovely face an' form."

"'Tisn't my duty to inspect a prisoner's face an' form for possible signs of nobility *or* divinity. My duty is to do as I'm told. And you ought to had thrown her down, like the Baroness said. Iffen she be an angel, she can fly, can't she?"

As they argued, I climbed down and soon the question was no longer worthy of dispute, as I had reached bottom. I trembled, however, for the Prince's fate.

When once I had stepped off the ladder, 'twas straightaway hauled up again and the trapdoor lowered.

I looked about me.

O! Several times during the course of this narrative you have seen me in great distress of mind and bewailing my fate, but never, I think, has my soul been so sunk in despond as at that moment of examining my accommodations in the State Dungeon of Breakabeen Castle.

If this was the detention cell for Very Important Prisoners, why then what could the cell for Prisoners of No Importance Whatsoever be like? 'Twas naught but a black hole in the ground. The walls were entirely sheer and impossible to scale; 'twould have been like trying to climb out of the bottom of a bottle.

There was no furniture: not a chair, not an old trunk, not even a projecting rock to sit upon. The only light came from a thin, thin slit cut through twelve feet of rock. Not the smallest bird, not even a butterfly, could have escaped through that slit. The air, as one might have expected, was stale. It smelled of mold and damp stones.

I wondered, did the Baroness mean to keep us alive for some purpose, or could her plans be achieved only by our deaths? 'Twould be easy enough to be rid of us by the simple expedient of withholding food and water. I preferred to read into the Baroness's behavior a desire to use our live persons in some ploy, presumably connected with her beloved, the King of Gilboa. In that event, I hoped that food and water would be shortly forthcoming, for I was beginning to feel a trifle faint.

In either case, there was naught to do but sit down patiently and begin picking with my teeth at the twine that bound my wrists together.

As I did so, my mind ranging over the many events of

the past few days, my heart was suddenly speared by the memory of my dearest Little Echo. Did you think I had forgot my injured Goose? In truth, I had for a time, in the swirl and march of events. But now I had all the leisure in the world to consider her danger.

When last I had examined her, she had seemed to be resting comfortably. I could only hope that our enforced stay here at the Castle of Breakabeen would do her good. She would have sufficient food for several days, for the bed she rested upon inside the Prince's saddlebags was made up of fresh green grass and herbs, just the sort of thing she liked to nibble upon. If the Prince were given water, I had no hesitation in believing that he would gladly give her all that she required.

I reflected that the Prince was a good sort of man, for all he was sometimes so silly.

'Twas many and many an hour before aught happened in that dark, silent place. But yet at length the trapdoor over my head opened and something was lowered to me on the end of a long cord. 'Twas a great fair loaf of bread, with a large hunk of cheese besides.

"Untie it," came the command from above.

I shielded my eyes to try to make out who addressed me, but 'twas of no avail. His head was against what to me appeared a very bright light and I could make out no details.

My hands now being free, I untied the bundle as instructed and the cord rose in the air and disappeared. After an interval a pitcher appeared in the opening and was lowered by the cord. On command, I untied the pitcher and once again the cord vanished.

Before the trapdoor could come crashing down, I spoke.

"I thank you for the food and drink," I said as my mother had taught me, and curtsied. There was little point in antagonizing whoever it was who brought me the means of survival.

The trapdoor hesitated in its arc and then dropped without another word spoken. Ah well. I was certain that they had heard me.

Most thankfully I made my meal. In my great hunger I ate nearly three-quarters of the bread and cheese, but the rest I retained for the morning after I had slept.

After a time the dim gray light in my prison chamber dimmed still more and turned to darkest black. I laid my head down on my sewing bag and composed myself for sleep.

How long I slept I cannot say, but the cell was once again filled with a thin gray light which gave no hint of the time of day. After eating, I looked about me for something with which to occupy myself.

I upended my sewing kit and examined the contents. Might I perhaps be able to fashion some sort of rope from my wedding gown? But then, even supposing I was able to tear the tough material (remember, I had no scissors anymore), what good would a rope do me? There was no way to attach it to the ceiling.

In the end, I tore out all the old sloppy seams and began to resew them with the finest, tiniest stitches I could manage in the low light, severing the thread with my teeth as required. 'Twas better to do aught than naught.

Five days went by. Or so I believe. I lost track somewhere after the third day, and could never after be certain which day I was on. My gown approached completion; indeed, to prolong the task, I added a good deal of embroidery around the neckline. Since it was executed in gold thread on a gold background, it did not show up to great advantage, but the task kept my mind from being wholly overthrown by the combination of boredom and terror which oppressed me.

A superstitious dread prevented me from finishing the dress. I feared that the moment I took the final stitch, the King of Gilboa and several prominent members of the clergy would instantaneously descend through the trapdoor to perform our wedding ceremony. I had, after all, given my word to marry when once the gown was done.

At last I put it aside and sought other occupation. 'Twas then that I remembered my talented, tricksy hair and resolved to put it to use.

Firstly I praised it and petted it and composed endless lines to its beauty, and then begged it to climb the wall and hitch itself to the rope ladder, a length of which remained inside the dungeon, while the greater part of it was drawn up through the trapdoor.

To give credit where credit is due, I must admit that the

hair tried. Nay, I cannot fault it on that account. But like many conceited creatures, it was not half so clever as it thought itself to be. In addition, I suppose it is true that the stuff had no organ of sight and had simply to feel its way about.

At first, I was quite pleased. It began to grow with a will and slowly poured itself out over the floor in a steady stream. I stood by, crying out such encouragement and commendations as occurred to me in my excitement. After a time, however, my enthusiasm dimmed somewhat, as it went on getting longer and longer and never gaining any altitude.

I decided to try to train it upwards, as one might train a fruit tree or grapevine up an orchard wall. I sat with my head pressed to the stone and pushed the tendrils of hair into the mortared joints. The hair seemed to understand the intention, but because the joints were so slender, it divided itself up into many strands instead of forming one strong lock. Furthermore, it still did not seem to have any sense of up, down, or sideways, but grew higgledy-piggledy every which way, so that had anyone been there to witness it, I should have been a truly terrifying sight. Indeed I would have put Medusa, that ancient Gorgon of Greece with the snakes growing out of her head, entirely in the shade.

Be that as it may, my serpentine hairstyle was of no practical use, and for a time I relapsed into gloom.

How long, I wondered idly, would my hair actually grow? I amused myself by imagining commanding it to grow and grow without cease until it overwhelmed the earth and threaded its locks through the deeps of the sea, strangling and choking all life therein. In my mind's eye I traced its progress, saw it slowly filling up the dungeon and spilling out over the top—

My thoughts suddenly focused on that picture. What, I wondered, would happen to me in that event? Should I be smothered to death in all that hair, or would I—could I—?

A plan darted into my head.

I must wait until after the next food delivery, which came but once a day. To my great relief, that delivery would come soon, or so I calculated by my sense of the passage of time. I did not believe that I could bear to wait much longer to try my idea.

After a small eternity, my bread, cheese, and water came. I thanked the anonymous bearer as usual, being careful not to allow any sense of my new hopefulness to creep into my speech. The trapdoor was duly lowered. Taking up my food and drink into my two hands and slinging my sewing kit over my shoulder, I began.

I repeated all the verses I could remember in praise of my hair and then begged it thusly:

"O my hair," I said, "thou hast labored long at my request this day. I now ask thee to do even more." My heart suddenly misgave me at the thought that what I asked might be too much on top of all the tomfoolery I had engaged in earlier, but I persisted. "I prithee, grow, and go on growing until I give thee leave to stop."

Obediently, the hair began to grow, and I began to pace slowly around the perimeter of the round room, allowing the hair to trail behind me on the ground. When once I had completed the circuit of the room, I must perforce tread upon my own hair, which I did.

Around and around I walked, my hair endlessly flowing out behind me and before me. I spoke kindly to my hair, honoring it for its energy and diligence as well as its great beauty.

Around and around and around. The path of my hair, which circled the room, grew gradually higher off the floor. I took a bite of bread and cheese as I walked and then a sip of water.

Around and around and around. I worried after a time that the golden pathway might become too slender and, lacking adequate support, cave in toward the center and pitch me to the ground. As I mounted higher and higher and the danger of such a fall became greater, I found it necessary to fix my eyes straight ahead, so that dread alone did not make me lose my balance.

Around and around and around. Would I never reach my destination? My hair was happily very thick, but when once I had walked upon it, 'twas compacted down much smaller. I was therefore raised up but a few inches with each revolution. It seemed I had been walking this shining trail all of my life. I dared not stop to rest, for the span of the road was not wide enough to allow me to sit or kneel with any security that I would ever be able to rise again. My voice grew hoarse with singing the praises of my tresses, and I was in the end reduced to a melancholy croaking like that of a raven.

"Good . . . hair. Very . . . very . . . wonderful . . ." I whispered, in barely audible tones. "Good . . . hair."

I dared not cease speaking my approval, for whenever I did so to drink a drop of water (the cheese and bread were long gone), the hair on the instant likewise ceased growing. I therefore went on, though few human listeners could have guessed at the meaning of my mumbles.

Around and around and around. I was growing clumsy through exhaustion of both mind and body. Eventually the ventilation slit was covered over and what light there had been vanished and the air grew foul. As the hours of darkness wound downward until dawn, I had to pinch myself very hard in order to stay awake. Even so, I fell into a sort of dream in which I thought that I was climbing the stairs within the Tower of Dorloo, mounting slowly up and up until my head would brush the roof of the tower—

Thunk!

I saw stars before my eyes and, in a daze, wondered if my head had somehow penetrated the tower roof and I now was gazing upon a starlit night. But I quickly regained my wits and realized that I had reached the top and had struck my head against the wooden floorboards of the castle basement.

I extended my right hand out toward the center of the

room. I could just barely see the length of rope ladder which remained inside the dungeon. I grasped at it.

I could not reach so far.

Nay, I could not. 'Twas no more than a handbreadth away from my groping fingers. Yet had I leaned ever so slightly more toward the center of the room I should have fallen to my death.

I wept. Far below I heard the clink and rattle as a rain of diamonds hit the stone floor. I considered flinging myself after my tears, to dash my brains out against that floor. What more was there to do, other than to die here atop a monstrous coil of my own hair, so close and yet so far from freedom?

I felt an odd tugging at my scalp, and shook my head impatiently, bracing myself to leap out into the air. I closed my eyes. What, I wondered, would the moment of impact be like?

Upon this thought I decided to wait and reflect further. While there is life there is yet hope. I opened my eyes again.

Something was happening along the length of the hair coil. It stirred and writhed in a terrifying manner, so that I was certain that its stability had eroded and the whole structure would sway and crash within a matter of moments. Then I saw that one strand, about the thickness of my thumb, was loosening itself from the mass. When it had freed itself, it deliberately shrank down until it was no more than a mere twenty feet long.

It hung there, doing nothing.

I stared at it.

"*What?*" I cried. "What am I to do with that strand of hair?"

There was no response, which was after all very much what might have been expected.

I reached out and took the lock of hair into my hand and considered. What I needed now was a sort of extension of my hand, to bridge the short distance between it and the ladder. I drew the hair up until I held near the end of it, a few fingerlengths protruding from my hand. I reached out once again to the rope ladder. The wisp of hair brushed the edge of it. Leaning perilously out over the void, I thrust it forward, let go and . . . hoped.

'Twas over the ladder rung!

I took a deep breath and said as clearly as I might, "Come to me, O my hair. Come to thy mistress who loves thee."

It came, sweet as a bird to the nest. It curled around the ladder rung and then returned to my hand.

And then, of course, all was easy.

I drew the ladder near, stepped onto it, interwove my arms in the ropes for security, and then pushed mightily upward on the trapdoor. In no time at all I was climbing out of my prison cell.

CHAPTER FOURTEEN

And Out Again

HAIR TODAY, GONE TOMORROW.
—PARAPHRASED PROVERB

*Y*ou, my quick-witted friend, will no doubt have foreseen my next trouble. 'Tis difficult to flee unseen and unheard down a castle corridor, even in the dark hours before dawn, while trailing gleaming golden tresses fully a mile long.

"I do most earnestly entreat you to decrease your length, O my hair," I whispered, but so far off were the nethermost ends of my curls that I could not judge if my command was being obeyed.

Furthermore, I had no idea where the other dungeon, holding the Prince and Little Echo, might be. I paused a moment for thought. My own dungeon had been cut out of the rock beneath one of the four towers of the inner keep. Might not the Prince and Little Echo be located in a cell beneath another tower?

I hurried on as best I could, dragging the heavy weight of my locks behind me. The sound of my hair following me,

145

nearly filling the wide halls, seemed like that of a mighty river to my frightened ears.

"Do diminish, dear hair, I pray you," I breathed. "I am sorry to hurry you, but I assure you that the task is urgent."

I gathered up great armfuls of the stuff in order to shorten my tail as much as possible, but yet I knew that the last of it might not leave the dungeon until well after I had quit the castle altogether. 'Twas almost as bad as being tied.

By the most prodigious luck I met no one and reached the next tower block safely. It seemed reasonable that those soldiers would have deposited the Prince in the nearest dungeon to mine; they were not the sort to exert themselves any more than necessary.

I found a trapdoor in the basement floor, opened it cautiously to avoid making any noise, and whispered: "Are you there? 'Tis I, Alexandria Aurora Fortunato, come to release you from this place of confinement."

A pause, then a quavering voice. "O, Yer Ladyship, is it really you come to get me? Indeed and you are an angel of mercy!"

"Smeatt?" I said, puzzled.

"That be my name, though 'twill always be a wonderment to me how yer came to know it, lady."

I paused for thought. "Do you know where my companion was incarcerated?"

Silence, then: "In-how-much, Yer Ladyship?"

"Where is my friend, do you know, Smeatt?" I asked.

"In the next tower block dungeon, I expect," said Smeatt. "But, wait, Yer Ladyship!" he wailed. "Y'won't be meaning to go away and leave me here, will ye? This do be the worst of all the dungeons, why, I wouldn't let 'em put yer friend 'ere, I made 'em take 'im along further. There's water in 'ere, with *things* swimmin' around.

"An' if ye leave me the Baroness will kill me sure, an' all because I did save Yer Ladyship's life, lo these many years ago. 'Tis not behavior fitten fer a great lady like yerself. I'll not believe it until I sees it."

"Of course I won't leave you here, Smeatt, not if you promise not to do anything to prevent our escape. But what do you mean, you saved my life long ago? I have never set eyes on you before, not until you found us in the forest these five days past."

Once again there was silence. Smeatt was thinking.

"How so be it iffen you let me out first and *then* I tells ye?"

I responded by throwing down the rope ladder to him.

"Ah! Yer a kind girl, you are, as I always—"

"Hush!" I whispered. "Explanations must wait until another time. I will go and get my companion. Do you," I asked, struck by a sudden thought, "know of a way out of this place?"

"As it so happens," said Smeatt, his head appearing over the edge of the trapdoor, "I believe I do, Yer Ladyship, if so be it as old customs still hold."

"I am overjoyed to hear it. Come along, Smeatt, come along. Ahead of me, if you please, or you will tread on my hair."

Smeatt was quite right. There was a third trapdoor in the third tower block (and a fourth in the fourth, for aught I know), and under it slept the Prince and Little Echo.

When once aroused by the rope ladder falling upon him, the Prince was quick enough in scrambling out, bearing Little Echo under one arm and the saddlebags over his shoulder.

"O!" I breathed when I saw her cradled in the crook of his elbow. "Is she — How is she?"

"Excellent well!" the Prince replied, smiling down upon her foolish little face with a doting expression. "Every day she gains a bit more ground. Why, today she flapped her wing — the injured one, you know, and —"

"Hush!" I whispered. "I beg your pardon, and I am more pleased than I can say, but we must be very, very quiet."

"Indeed, that is so," said the Prince, sobering. His eyes lit upon on my hair, which wound away down the corridor and around the corner. "Alas!" he murmured, pointing to it. "Not again!"

"Nay, 'tis not fastened anywhere, but 'twill require the passage of some time before 'tis again of a manageable length. Smeatt," I said, turning to the soldier, "I pray you, lead us out of this castle, if you can."

"Right this way then, Yer Ladyship and sir."

The way out of the castle appeared to be a doorway so tiny as to appear that it was made for dwarfs, which led down to the river. As Smeatt had predicted, it opened silently at a touch.

The Prince was inclined to be critical.

"Why, Smeatt, is this door unlocked? 'Tis a most unwarrantable violation of the proper security of this castle."

Smeatt became evasive. "'Tis the usual procedure, like."

"But why is it the usual procedure?"

"O well now, I couldn't exactly say. But where's the harm? True, we do be at war at the present time, but"—he tittered, as though at a vastly witty jest—"'tain't as though the Prince of Dorloo were standin' right outside with 'is army, is 'ee now? Like as not, 'ee's off canoodlin' with 'is girl somewheres, so what's the point in bein' over particular?"

"Smeatt," began the Prince sternly, and I had once again to warn them to lower their voices.

"There be nothin' wrong in a few of the lads slippin' off downstream to Clove City to see their sweet'earts an' drink a few ales, be there?" argued Smeatt. "An' the door gots to be left open so as they can slide back in afore dawn, y'see."

"Nothing wrong?" the Prince exploded. "Smeatt, I am shocked—!"

"Hist!" I hissed.

Somewhat abashed, the Prince contented himself with training a sad, reproachful look upon Smeatt, which made the soldier squirm as though he had a tunic full of ants.

Considering that, had the door *not* been left unlocked,

149

we three should no doubt be shortly discovered and clapped into irons if not worse, it appeared to me that there was no great need to make such ado about the matter. However, 'twas not worth discussion and I kept silent as we passed through.

I had only just stepped through the door and put one foot out of the castle when I felt a sudden sharp pull on my hair. I caught at the Prince's arm.

"Someone has taken hold of my hair," I gasped.

He turned to me, concerned. "What should we do, Mistress Alexandria?"

"Help me to carry it along. O, we must run!"

The Prince and Smeatt on each side of me flung their arms around my hair and tugged. We stumbled along as quickly as we might down toward the river. A tremendous barking arose behind us in the castle.

"There used to be some boats tied up down 'ere," panted Smeatt, and when we reached the riverside there was, verily, a small boat tethered to a willow tree.

My hair seemed to grow heavier and heavier with each step I took. I imagined at least a score of soldiers hauling on it.

"Into the boat, lady," cried Smeatt, as he and the Prince heaved the mass of my hair down the bank. I needed no urging, but climbed in as swiftly as I could scramble, followed by the Prince and Smeatt.

"Push off," I cried. "Push off into the current!" The Prince and Smeatt, each taking an oar, did so, and as they did so, the end of my hair came into sight through the door in the wall.

My hair had been steadily shrinking, at my request, and was now no longer than an eighth of a mile. On it rode a Sergeant with great braided shoulder pads and a high hat, three foot soldiers, four barking dogs, and five dirty children. All of the last-named nine individuals appeared to be under the impression that this was some sort of entertainment expressly designed for their amusement. Both children and dogs lost their balance periodically and rolled hilariously about before regaining their footing. They yelped and shrieked with joy. The soldiers were less pleased with this diversion and held on grimly, as one might cling to the mane of a horse.

Never could we three have pulled this mighty weight along, had my hair not been helping. Still, our great peril required an even greater deed. I stood up in the boat, provoking protests from both Smeatt and the Prince.

"O my hair," I cried out in a clear, ringing voice, "thou who art the greatest wonder of the Western World, thou crowning glory of glories, O thou hair beyond compare, come to me, I pray thee, that I may pet thee and comb thee and tender thee thy full mead of praise. Come to me . . . NOW!"

'Twas a mistake to have stood up in the boat.

I never precisely saw what happened. The others told

me, however, that my hair snapped back to my head with a speed too rapid for the eye to follow. I promptly plunged into the river. All the assorted soldiers, children, and dogs, having had the rug snatched out from under their feet (so to speak), rolled merrily down the hill like so many cartwheels and eventually came to rest, some on the bank and some in the water.

"Were any drowned?" I asked some time later, after I had been dragged back on board, at considerable risk to the stability of the rowboat, and revived from my unconscious state.

"Nay, worse luck," said Smeatt.

"Nay, mistress, do not fear," said the Prince, gently mopping my face dry with one of the little Goose gowns from my sewing bag. "The children and dogs bounced right back up again none the worse for their ride, only vexed to find it come to an end. And the soldiers only fell in knee-deep water, so all were well."

"And Little Echo?"

"Is well," said the Prince, smiling.

"And you? And Smeatt?"

"All, all are well. And here is your comb, for I believe you made a solemn promise not twenty minutes past, which it would be proper to now fulfill."

And so I sat in the bow of the boat and combed my hair in the rays of early morning sunlight which were now breaking over the hill. The gold dust fell about us like a gilded rain and was like to have swamped the boat, had Smeatt not offered to scoop it out into the stream.

Sweetly did I sing songs to my tresses such as I remembered my mother to have sung to me as a babe; I kissed my locks and called them by pet names and recited nonsense rhymes in their honor. I was well content to do so, for I owed them my life and liberty and would not soon forget my debt.

The Prince and Smeatt took turns rowing the boat. Sometimes they allowed it to be borne along, as we were in the current of a deep, mud-bottomed river, and it drew us along right speedily.

As if to crown my joy, just as I was about to drift off to sleep, a gaggle of eleven white Geese appeared overhead, circled, and then landed, splash! splash! splash! around us. Little Echo honked excitedly, the Prince laughed for pleasure, and Smeatt stealthily drew out a small slingshot from within his tunic and began to grope for something with which to arm it.

"Lay down your weapon, Smeatt," said the Prince. "These are our friends, not our dinner."

Smeatt was dubious. "Them there are birds, sir and madam. Geese, or so I believe. Commonly grown for their eggs, meat, and feathers. One of 'em alone would make a fine meal an' 'ere we got eleven of 'em. Twelve, counting that one in yer bag there."

"Come, Smeatt," said the Prince mildly. "Know now that

it you so much as harbor a covetous thought about these birds we shall instantly fling you overboard to sink or swim. We shall find another meal."

The Prince seemed changed in character since his stay in the Baroness's dungeons. He struck me as older, less giddy in the brains. Why this should be, I could not say.

Having no food to offer, he yet leaned forward and held out his hand to my Geese. They pressed forward and affectionately nibbled at his fingers in a manner that nearly (I say, *nearly*) made me jealous.

I leaned back and closed my eyes, content to listen to my Geese splashing about me, refreshing themselves with a quick bath and a nibble of water weed.

"Where are we going?" I asked drowsily, feeling that I ought to give at least some part of my mind to our current predicament.

"Down river," responded the Prince. "You see, all rivers flow downhill to the sea, and therefore that is the direction the current is taking us. If we were to remain in this boat for many days, we should at length come out upon the Saltine Sea."

"I am acquainted with the basic facts of geography, Your Highness," I said, feeling too content to be as annoyed with the Prince as usual. Indeed, it occurred to me that I would not like him to grow so wise as to become unrecognizable; I had grown accustomed to him as he was. "But what human habitation shall we meet along the way?" I asked.

The Prince frowned. "Well," he said, "just around this

bend, I believe, lies Clove City, where —" he shifted his gaze to Smeatt, who abruptly fell to studying his fingernails — "our friend here and his companions were wont to disport themselves in the middle of the night.

"Then there are a number of small towns alongside the riverbank whose names I do not know. 'Tis mayhap twenty miles downstream from here that we shall fetch up against Roseboom."

"Roseboom?" I opened my eyes. "Roseboom, the capital city of Gilboa, where the King's castle is?"

"That is correct, mistress."

"And how fast do you suppose we are moving now?"

The Prince screwed up his eyes, scrutinized the passing shoreline, and stroked a nonexistent beard thoughtfully like a wise old man of the sea. "Two knots, I should think, or a bit more when we row," he said at last.

"And what," I asked, "does that mean in practical terms? How long before we find ourselves swept up (figuratively speaking in your case, literally in mine), into the King's embrace?"

The Prince opened his eyes rather wide at that.

"'Twould be about . . . why about three hours before nightfall this evening."

"Just in time for supper," I said grimly. "At what hour, I wonder, do they dine at the castle? I am getting rather hungry."

At that moment we rounded the bend and saw the houses and church steeples of Clove City spread out ahead of us. It occurred to me that Smeatt had been rowing us very close to shore.

"Ah!" said Smeatt, with every sign of satisfaction as he saw the town appear. "Here, my dear sir and madam, is where I do be leaving yer."

CHAPTER FIFTEEN

On the River

'TIS AN ILL WIND THAT BLOWETH
NO MAN TO GOOD.
    — JOHN HEYWOOD, PROVERBS

The Prince and I were both so surprised by this sudden defection that Smeatt very nearly got away unchallenged. In truth, the man was nimbler on his toes than I would ever have given him credit for — he was half out of the boat ere I snagged the back of his collar.

"So ho, Smeatt!" I cried, hauling him back into the boat by the simple expedient of half strangling him with his own neckband. "Whither away so speedily? I'faith, I think it most discourteous of you. Here we are, simply longing to hear your tale in full. Would you leave us in ignorance?"

For it had quite suddenly come to me that there were several facts about Smeatt which had yet to be explained.

"Didn't think a fine lady like yer'd be interested in the doin's of a 'umble man like meself," gasped Smeatt, clutching at his collar. "Could yer — gak! Could yer leave go of me, milady? Me head is almost twisted right off."

"Indeed, Mistress Alexandria," said the Prince, musing, "I

did not think on it before, but 'tis strange that Smeatt should also have been imprisoned. Why was it so?" he asked Smeatt.

"Dunno," muttered Smeatt.

"Come, man," said the Prince, beginning to get that look in his eye which invariably seemed to intimidate Smeatt, for all that the Prince was little more than a boy. "Did she give *no* reason? What did the guards say when they put you into the dungeon?"

Smeatt's eyes shifted back and forth, seeking escape. The Prince and I instantly each gripped one of his arms and then awaited results.

"She sent a message," he eventually admitted. "She said: 'Tell Smeatt that he should have killed them all.'"

"Killed them all?" I repeated, puzzled. "But whom *did* you kill?"

"*Nobody.* Nobody! I didn't kill none of 'em. An' now one of 'em's got to show up in the flesh an' make me look bad in front of the Baroness. Why couldn't yer have stayed in Dorloo where y'belong? Didn't even know ye were one of 'em at first but I expect y'are; one of the little 'uns, ye would be, all growed up."

"One of *what* little ones?"

"Little *girls*, o' course," bawled Smeatt, nearly in tears. "Hundreds of 'em, there were. All screechin' an' bellyachin' fit to bust a gut. Gave me a headache, it did. I gots sensitive ears. An' there be the lady on 'er knees, prayin', and the little girls all yowlin' like a pack o' wildcats. *Naturally* I didn't kill nobody. I'm a kindly soul, I am. Why, I even saw 'em safe to the border of Dorloo, an' waved goodbye to 'em nice as pie." He paused, his chest heaving with affronted virtue.

"An' now I'll be goin'," he said suddenly and twisted, agile as an eel, out of our grasp and out of the boat.

"Nay!" I cried. "Beshrew me if I allow you to leave it at that!" and I leapt out into the water after him.

"Hi!" shouted the Prince, the boat rocking madly with all this activity.

The water was only chest high, but I was hampered by my long gown. Still, he also seemed to be floundering and I managed to throw my arms around his waist. An immediate explosion of gold dust into the river revealed the reason for his sluggish movements; every pocket was weighted down with the heavy metal. However hard he struggled, I refused to let him go. The Geese clustered about and bit him and the Prince smacked him smartly on the skull with one of the oars and cried: "Halt, sirrah, and explain yourself!"

Finally Smeatt shouted, "I yield! Let me go and I'll give it back!"

Surprised, I slackened my grip a little.

"Here! Here it be! Take it back!"

He rummaged about on his person and then thrust something small and cold into my hand.

"I ain't got the rest o' the jewels no more so there be no point in askin' fer 'em. An' I see you gots the crown already, so that's it. We do be quits. Now let me go!" And with a violent wrench which tipped me over onto the muddy bottom, he escaped my hold and lurched up out of the water and onto the bank, the Geese screaming and flapping in pursuit.

Over the sloshing of water and indignant shrieks of the Geese we could hear wafted back to us on the wind: "Sor-r-e-e-e, lay-d-e-e-e!"

Having swallowed a goodly quantity of water, I was in no position to join the chase. Coughing and sputtering, I struggled back to the boat and rested for a moment, hanging onto the gunwale. When I had recovered, I towed the rowboat closer to shore where I might more easily board. The Geese returned without Smeatt as I clambered inside, wet to the skin for the second time in an hour.

"What did he give you?" the Prince inquired.

Rather curious about that myself, I opened my hand. On it lay a golden ring with a very large ruby embedded in it. The Prince and I stared at it for a moment in silence, mystified.

"He said something about your crown," said the Prince slowly. "'Tis true enough that ruby jewelry does seem to be seeking you out of late. First a crown, then a necklace, now a ring. Where do you suppose he got this ring?"

Scornfully I curled my lip. "From the sound of it, I should say that some unfortunate lady gave it to him to prevent him from murdering her and her charges."

The Prince looked up at me. "I know naught of your family, Mistress Alexandria, save that they are dead. Could this lady have been your mother, and you one of the children?"

I shook my head. "Nay. 'Tis a case of mistaken identity. I

160

was born in that small cottage where you and the King found me, and never ventured farther away than ten or twelve miles at most in all the years of my life before you took me to the tower. So my mother told me, and so I remember. Besides, who were the other children? I am the only child of my parents.

"Methinks the lady was a governess with her pupils, perchance," I continued. "According to Smeatt's tale there were too many to have been the lady's daughters. They were no doubt the offspring of several families, all being taught by the same schoolmistress. Where she obtained the ring I cannot say, but mayhap it belonged to one of her students who was of noble birth."

"Put it on," urged the Prince.

"No, sire, 'tis not mine. I wonder what happened to the poor young lady who bought her life with it? It ought to be on her finger, not mine. I will not wear it."

Little Echo, who had up to this moment been sitting quietly on the Prince's lap, now started up an enormous ado.

"Kee-wonk! Kee-wonk! Kee-wonk!" she called, sounding more like a braying donkey than a well-bred Goose.

"What is it, Little Echo? Does aught pain you?" asked the Prince, bending tenderly over her and stroking her ruffled feathers.

At this Little Echo seemed to become even more agitated. She went so far as to hiss at the Prince, who laughed and said, in a sickening falsetto voice, "And is it in a naughty temper? Does it want to— Ow! *Bad* girl! No biting!"

161

"Let me look at her wound," I said, slipping the ring into my bag, where I could hear it clink against the twelve Goose crowns. Little Echo, however, was yet behaving like a spoilt little awp and 'twas something of a tussle before I was able to examine her damaged wing.

"It looks much better," I was saying, when the Prince interrupted.

"Hush," he said. "Look there."

We were at present drifting past Clove City. 'Twas a town of fair size and population. Beyond it loomed an enormous hulk which looked disturbingly familiar. I groaned.

"But we have been traveling for hours!" I protested. "That cannot be the Castle of Breakabeen."

"I ought to have realized," the Prince said somberly. "A town of the magnitude of Clove City would never have been situated so far away from the castle which protects it. We have been occupied for the past hour and a half, for 'tis no longer, I believe, in rounding this great spit of land around which the river flows. We are scarcely more than half an hour on foot from the castle. I wondered why no one seemed to be pursuing us by water. They had only to cross the neck of the headland in order to cut us off."

I was silent, scanning the shoreline for evidence that this last statement was true.

I reached out a cold, damp hand and touched the Prince's.

"O look there," I whispered.

There were soldiers on the wharf that jutted out into the

river, and they were speedily piling into boats. But that is not all that chilled my blood. Behind the sailors, in a long line, were posts rising up eight feet from the ground, normally used for the drying and mending of fishing nets. And on each post, suspended from large iron hooks, dangled a hanged man. Or woman. 'Twas too distant to tell the sex.

"Row!" commanded the Prince. "Sit you down next to me and we will row together, using all our might. They will come up with us in an instant, if we do not make haste."

With a will, I flung myself down on the bench beside him and gripped the oar in both hands.

"Ready?" asked the Prince. "*Down* stroke!"

We found our rhythm quickly and rowed as smooth as silk together; the little boat seemed to leap over the waves. Alas! 'Twas in vain. However swiftly we moved, our pursuers moved yet more swiftly. One boat possessed several sets of oarlocks and several rowers, and another raised a sail.

"Smeatt knew this," I grunted, as my oar dug deep into the river. "No wonder he wished to leave us before we came abreast of Clove City. So much for his fine words."

"'Tis not worth thinking of, Mistress Alexandria," said the Prince calmly. "'Tis the sort of man he is, that is all."

"True," I assented. "What shall we do?" The other boats were approaching fast.

"Whatever we must," answered the Prince. "One thing you shall *not* do is to attempt to save me at your own expense. 'Twill not serve and I shall not permit it. Do you understand me?"

"I do, my lord," I said meekly. A spirit of mischief over-
came me, even at this grave moment. "What," I gasped out
as we swung our oars overhead, "became of your promise to
obey me in all things?"

"Release me then from my bond, for I will otherwise fling
myself into the river to be drowned or speared like a fish,
rather than do aught that would harm you, mistress."

"You are released, then," I said, privately thinking that his
bond had not been worth a great deal, thus far. And yet I
would not have said so for all the world, for I was much
moved by his words.

They overtook us in a matter of moments. We offered no
resistance; it seemed pointless. I had no desire to get wetted
through once again, and there truly was no hope for escape.
In any case, I was tired of escaping. 'Twas all I seemed to be
doing lately.

The two lead boats surrounded us, one on each side. A
soldier climbed gingerly into our boat and tied us up once
again, this time both hand and foot. Rather than attempt to
convey our trussed-up bodies into one of their boats, they
made our boat fast to both of theirs and towed us along, the
soldier remaining with us to help speed our journey by
rowing.

To my surprise, we did not head for Clove City and those
dreadful dangling corpses, but rather continued on downstream.

"Where are we going?" I asked the soldier when once our
direction had become evident.

Like most of his kind, he disliked being questioned by a prisoner. He looked at me briefly and then away, rowing hard. When I persisted, he reluctantly replied: "Roseboom," and snapped shut his mouth, merely shaking his head when I inquired further.

"The King," I murmured softly to the Prince, "will certainly be with his army in Dorloo, will he not? I wonder why they bring us to Roseboom."

The Prince shook his head. "The Baroness no doubt summoned him back to Gilboa when she realized who we were. We are prisoners of some importance, I fear. Important enough to warrant the King's personal attention."

So we were, then, to be taken before the King.

CHAPTER SIXTEEN

In Which We Travel to the King's Court

A PENNY FOR YOUR THOUGHT.
— JOHN HEYWOOD, *PROVERBS*

*O*ur craft moved swiftly downstream, ever closer to the great city of Roseboom and the King's castle. The Prince took my bound hands in his and I will confess that I derived some comfort from that fact, for I was sore afraid. We did not speak, but sat gazing out at the sunlit lands which slowly uncurled and stretched out before us. When once this river journey was done, I doubted that we should either of us ever see daylight again. I had escaped the King once and he was unlikely to allow me to do so a second time. And as for the Prince—

Until the King's treasury was filled to bursting with riches, until not one more thimbleful of gold dust or diamonds could be crammed in howsoever hard the King's seneschals tried, there was ample reason to keep me alive. What reason was there for keeping the Prince alive? Why, none at all. Nay, there was every reason to send him to his death, and the sooner the better.

The Queen of Dorloo was long since dead and the King of Dorloo was ailing. As rumor had it and the Prince had confirmed, his father was addled in his brains. Naught save the Prince's life stood in the way of the prompt annexation of Dorloo into Gilboa.

My hands tightened on the Prince's.

"My father is dead," he murmured. "Did you know?"

"No!" I cried.

"They told me of it on the second day in the dungeon. He died of an apoplectic fit, it seems, when his ministers were at last able to make him understand that the King's army was battering at the very castle gates and that no one knew where I was."

I was silent for a moment. Then I said, "Mayhap they lie. It might not be true."

He frowned and whispered fiercely, "I *want* it to be true."

Startled, I turned and stared at my gentle Prince.

"But why, sire?"

"Otherwise the King of Gilboa would have dragged him out and humiliated him in front of our people before executing him. As 'tis, they have displayed his severed head on a pike over the castle gatehouse." He flinched and closed his eyes. A single tear trickled down his cheek. "He was very good to me always, even in these last few years, when as like as not he did not recognize me. He was a kind man."

We sat quiet, watching my Geese swimming serenely alongside us.

"Now he need never have to live with the knowledge that he fathered a fool," said the Prince.

"O, sire, you must not—"

"Must I not?" he demanded. "I think I must."

A load of guilt settled like an iron band over my heart.

"If 'twere not for me—" I began.

Irritably the Prince cast my hands away. "'Twas naught to do with you. Or almost naught." He recaptured one of my hands and stroked it absentmindedly. "'Twas but a boy's prank, going off after you without telling anyone what I was doing. I was sick to my very gizzard with old Pennyfavor and the Code of Chivalry and the duties of a King. The old twiddlepoop hasn't let me out of his sight for three years, not since my father's wits went wandering. That day, the day that you flew away, was the first time in years I had escaped my minders. 'Twas glorious freedom to be out in the woods alone, unmarked by other eyes, at least until darkness fell and I found myself in a strange land alone."

He smiled rather wanly at me. "So you must not blame yourself. You never asked me to follow you, did you?"

I had had that very thought less than a week ago. Yet now it seemed to me that I was in the wrong, all the same.

"You will make a fine Queen of Gilboa and Dorloo, Mistress Alexandria." He smiled again. "If, that is, you can circumvent the plots and schemes of the King's intended bride. If I were a betting man, I would be glad to wager all I own that yourself rather than the Baroness of Breakabeen will win out in the end. I only grieve that I shall not be here to watch you wipe up the floor with Her Ladyship. You are a woman of character, mistress. I did not truly value what I was pursuing until now, when I have lost you for once and for all."

"Stop, I pray you," I whispered. "Do not speak so. Remember how we escaped in the valley of the Ogresses. Remember how we escaped from the dungeons of Castle Breakabeen. Mayhap we will also escape from the castle of the King."

"Mayhap we will." His eyes blinked, fighting off tears. He lifted his bound hands up to finger the curls of my hair. "'Tis most amazing stuff," he said, shaking his head in wonderment. "As is its mistress."

We lapsed into silence once more, and for some time watched the countryside passing by, without comment.

There was some cause for comment, however. 'Twas a lovely land, but something had gone wrong with it. Golden sunlight fell on broad acres which had not yet been plowed and planted, although 'twas June. Weeds grew, rank and wild, over grape arbors, choking and smothering the good vines. Bony cattle roamed untended and unchecked, eating the few tender young crop plants that sprouted from the fields. At intervals we saw grim lines of dangling corpses such as we had first seen in Clove City. There were many habitations, both sizable communities and lonesome farmhouses, as I had observed when flying over with my Geese, but they appeared to be in bad repair and some were blackened with the brand of fire.

At length I could hold my peace no longer. "What ails the people of this country? Are they mad to let their land go to rack and ruin?"

"They are mad, yes, but only with grief, or so I think," said the Prince. "The King's rule has been harsh in these past fourteen years. There are fewer to till the soil and tend the beasts, and those that remain are sick at heart and have little joy in their toil."

"Why do you say, 'in the past fourteen years'? I was born but fourteen years ago and am therefore ignorant of events before that time."

"I was myself but a babe at the time and can tell you little save that prior to that time this country was ruled over by another and more kindly sovereign. The man you know as the King of Gilboa was then no more than a Baron, the Baron of Dwelly and Zeh, which Barony is located quite near that of Breakabeen. No doubt that is why he and the Baroness were early affianced. He does not seem to have taken that promised union very seriously, by the by, as he has married and buried two wives already, neither of them the Baroness."

"But what happened to the other King?" I asked.

"Brutally butchered," said the Prince in a melancholy tone. "There was a family too, I understand. All killed by the Baron of Dwelly and Zeh, or those in his pay."

I shivered and fell silent, meditating upon the character

of the man that I was to wed in such short order. However, as harsh as my fate was likely to be, it could not compare with that facing the Prince. I tried to think of aught that would divert him as we drew moment by moment closer to his doom.

"Tell me," I said, tucking my hand through his arm, "about your father in the years before his illness."

He spoke to me of his father's goodness, of his great concern for the welfare of his people, and of his unfortunate weakness for staging, and engaging in, tournaments. "'Twas a tournament three years ago that was his downfall, for he was felled by a mighty blow which cleaved him open to the very brain pan. He lived, but never truly recovered in body or mind."

When the Prince's words finally faltered to a halt, I began to speak affectionately of my own mother, and then of the years lived on my own alone in the little cottage in the wood.

And so the bright hours passed one by one. The great orb of the sun reached its zenith and declined. And when the shadows began to streak across the fields and meadows, we came at last to Roseboom and the King's castle.

"You had best take Little Echo when we get out of the boat," said the Prince. "She is not fit to be on her own and I will not long be able to care for her."

"Yes, sire," I said, and tried to take her from him. The silly little Goose struggled and would not come to me, however.

"Mayhap you should carry her as long as you can. She does not seem to wish to leave you."

I turned to speak to the other Geese, sitting up in the boat as best I could.

"O my clever and beautiful ones," I said. "My dear friends and companions. We must bid you adieu, for the place we are going is not a healthy locale for such as thee." Or, I thought, for such as we, but I did not trouble myself to speak the thought aloud. "If you linger in this place for some days, I hope to find a way to return your sister Little Echo to you, when she is healed of her hurt. Fare thee well and go thy ways in happiness and peace."

I waited. Naught happened. The foolish little fizgigs went swimming along next the boat as though I had never spoken.

"Go!" I said sharply. "Leave us! You have never been laggardly before in taking to wing when danger threatened! So go now!"

"Mistress Alexandria! Do not be so unkind," said the Prince as the boat thumped against the quay and two soldiers jumped out to make it fast. "They do not wish to desert you. Do not abuse them so."

We were hauled, none too gently, out of the boat and laid like cargo on the dock. From this position 'twas difficult to see what was happening, but I heard someone approach and speak in a low tone to one of our captors. We were thereupon dragged to our feet and our ankle bonds released. My

Geese joined us upon the quay and followed us in two straight lines as we marched up the long, long ramp from the riverside in through the castle gate. Little Echo, who was surely well enough to walk with her sisters, did not, but rather remained clasped in the Prince's arms.

The Castle of Roseboom was a very different affair from the Castle of Breakabeen. I did not wish to admit it, even to myself, but the great stone building in which we found ourselves was an imposing residence.

Vaulted ceilings soared so high over our heads that the top was hazy with distance. Gigantic tapestries, which must each have cost whole lifetimes to complete, hung on the walls, glowing with jewel-like hues. These were interspersed with innumerable colored banners which lifted and fluttered in the breeze blowing in off the river through the large high windows. A U-shaped banquet table, fifty feet long and fifty feet wide, filled the room. A multitude of servants scurried about, preparing for the evening meal.

The Prince looked about him and smiled rather wanly. "By my fay, mistress, methinks you are getting the better part of the bargain in marrying the King after all. I have naught like so fine a house in which to receive you."

I sniffed. "O, I don't know," I said, pretending to a disdain which I did not in fact feel. "These rushes underfoot are not of the freshest. And that table needs dusting."

We were conducted through the great banqueting room and on to the throne room, which was an equally impressive chamber. And 'twas no less striking for containing a large group of handsomely attired people, clustered about the King of Gilboa, who was seated upon his golden throne.

"Aaaah," sighed the King with deep satisfaction as we came to a halt before him. "Here are they at last before me: my bride and my enemy, all tied up in ribands and bows, as pretty a present as any man could ask for."

CHAPTER SEVENTEEN

The Castle of the King

A STITCH IN TIME SAVES NINE.
—PROVERB

"Your Royal Highness," I said, curtsying deeply.

The Prince merely inclined his head. He did not seem anxious to pacify the King.

The King smiled. 'Twas a smile so wicked it took my breath away. His good humor made him no more attractive as a marital prospect.

"You really cannot imagine," he said, "how deeply I am indebted to you both. How very *kind* of you to turn up like this and save me the trouble and expense of searching for you. And both together, too; so convenient. I must say, I'm quite overwhelmed."

"A substantial ransom will of course be offered for my return, and for the return of this lady, unharmed, to Dorloo," said the Prince coldly. We both knew that there was little chance of the King taking up this offer, but it had to be made.

"Quite unnecessary, I assure you, as your little country is now a part of Gilboa. And as our countries are now one, there is need only for one ruler. Too many Kings cause confusion, you know."

We said naught. It occurred to me that the Prince was no longer a Prince since his father's death, but a King.

"I see that my bride has brought along her entourage. These ladies, I assume"— the King of Gilboa gestured at the Geese, who had followed us into the throne room and were looking about with apparent interest — "are your attendants. Is that not so, my dear?"

"They are my most dearly beloved Geese, sire."

"I see. Pardon my criticism, beloved, but while you are no less lovely than memory led me to believe, you are somewhat less neat and orderly in your attire. To speak crudely, both you and your companion give the appearance of having been rolled in a muck heap in the not-too-distant past."

I looked down at my torn dress and then over at the Prince (I could not help but think of him as the Prince). 'Twas true enough that we were less than tidy. Mud stained both my gown and his white suit. River weed clung to the jagged hem of my dress and also snaked down one of his legs into his boot. His Highness was in addition clutching a large bird under one arm. None of this enhanced our dignity.

"We have had little leisure for personal grooming, sire," I conceded.

"We must remedy that lack," said the King. "I believe I once remarked that that very gown you are wearing was more than adequate for your wedding day. I say so no longer. I'll not have such a ragged tatterdemalion stand beside me as my wedded wife. Let me think. Do I not recall that your wedding garments, upon which you toiled for so long, were carried in that bag which you have on your arm? Come, let me see what is inside."

I hesitated, but seeing that there was no help for it, I reluctantly approached and handed the King my bag. He took it and unceremoniously turned it upside down, dropping the contents on the ground before him. I bit my lip to see the little crowns rolling about on the stone floor, but held my tongue.

"What the devil—?" he said, holding up one of the Goose gowns.

"They are—" I faltered. "They belong to my Geese. As do the little crowns."

The King's smile grew wider and wider, until he looked like naught but a gnarled old crocodile. "By my oath, the Goose Girl plays at dolls and poppets with those mangy old birds. Very well, your Geese shall attend your wedding in their festive apparel and make merry with us. 'Tis only fair, after all: tonight we provide *them* with a feast, for soon enough they shall be providing *us* with a feast."

I swallowed but remained silent.

"And what are these?" He held out the ruby necklace and ring, and my crown, which I had removed while I combed my hair. The light from the high windows beamed down on them and bathed us in a crimson glow. The gems seemed larger than they had when I last laid eyes upon them.

The King turned them over in his hands. "These are a dowry well worth having, Goose Girl. The crown I recognize as one you were wont to wear. Whence came the others?"

"They are not mine, sire."

"Nonsense. Then they are mine, since I have found them here in my own hall, and I give them to you as a bride gift. I wish you to wear them tonight."

I bowed my head. The King seemed struck by my ruby crown; he looked from it to the other jewelry in his hand and frowned. "I have not seen rubies like these for many years," he murmured to himself. Then he shrugged his shoulders and returned to his perusal of my belongings.

"Ah! And here is the fabled golden wedding gown. Have you finished it yet, Goose Girl?"

"Not quite, sire."

"What do you mean? Look," he said, shaking it out and holding it up before him like a dressmaker displaying her goods. "'Tis quite perfect now, and neatly sewn, to boot."

"There remains three inches of the hem, my lord. Allow me to show you." I stooped and lifted the hem for his inspection.

"Then sit down and finish it, Goose Girl. You said, did you not, that you would marry when it was completed? We will wait while you do so."

A manservant hurried forward with a chair and I sank into it. I held up my bound hands to show that I could not sew thus tied; the King nodded and the servant cut my fetters off.

"I have no scissors," I protested.

"Get them," he ordered the servant.

We waited in silence as the man departed to procure the necessary tool. When he returned and handed me the scissors I opened my mouth once again.

"Sire, I cannot complete the task until—"

"That will do, Goose Girl. Finish the dress. At once."

As there was naught else to be done, I threaded my needle and commenced sewing. This time I used the tiniest stitches I could manage, but all the same, 'twas over in no time at all. At the last, however, I did not knot the thread but left it loose and contrived to pull out the last stitch as I lowered the hem to the floor. I intended to try to avoid this marriage to the bitter end, and if by any chance I was successful, I did not wish for anyone to claim that I had broke my bond.

"Excellent," said the King. "Now go and prepare for your wedding. And take those animals with you."

I looked over at the Prince. The King's glance followed mine, then flicked to the soldiers who had escorted us.

"Take him out and kill him," said the King. "Display the head for the people to see."

The Prince's expression did not alter, but his whole form stiffened.

I sank to my knees before the King.

"I beg you, sire, not to do this. If there is aught that I may do that will persuade you to spare his life, be assured, I will do it. Anything, Your Highness, anything at all."

"It grieves me to refuse such a pretty request, but refuse it I must. However, if it pleases you to have your swain cling to life until after your wedding, I see no reason against it. Take him to the dungeon," he said to the soldiers, "there to await execution when I give the word."

Relieved to have won for the Prince at least this small reprieve, I turned to go. Even the King could hardly send his soldiers in to guard me while I bathed. Mayhap I might climb unobserved out of my window and do—well, whatever I might.

"I have another little gift for you, Goose Girl," said the King slyly. "Another attendant, who may be of more practical use than your Geese. There is a lady whom I wish to honor by making her your lady-in-waiting. I can imagine no greater proof of my esteem, or aught that would better please her."

He nodded once again at the manservant, who this time went to the door, opened it, and ushered in . . . the Baroness.

"Your . . . Your Ladyship," I said when I had recovered my composure. I began to curtsy but the King forestalled me.

"Tut tut, Goose Girl. You must not curtsy to the Baroness, but she to thee. You rank above her now."

With a look that longed to melt my flesh like butter in a

bakery on a hot summer's day, the Baroness dipped her knees perhaps half an inch.

"The Baroness is my childhood sweetheart, you know. You ladies will no doubt have a pleasant gossip, as I am told that females like to do when their men are not about."

He turned to the Baroness. "And you, my dear, will be sure to keep a rather closer eye on my pretty little lamb, will you not? I lost her once when she was in your keeping, and I could not bear to do so again."

The Baroness met his eye with a look as freezing cold as the one she had bestowed upon me had been blistering hot. She did not reply but just barely nodded her head. No love was lost there, thought I. 'Twas ambition only made her wish to be his wife.

We were all now marched off to our separate accommodations, the Prince to the dungeon and my Geese, the Baroness, and I to the Queen's chambers. The Prince still had Little Echo, I realized, and I reached out my arms to take her. The Prince smiled at me as he handed her to me. 'Twas a smile that made my heart feel curiously tight in my chest, as though 'twere about to burst. I swallowed a sob and went onward. I held Little Echo in a grip of steel, for the bird was making a foolish fuss.

When once we had reached the Queen's quarters, a soldier opened the door for us and ushered us in. In an apparent attempt to relieve her feelings at least a little, the Baroness grasped me roughly by the arm and thrust me inside. I broke away and, lifting my skirts and calling to my

Geese, ran into the inner room, where a steaming, scented bath and three startled maidservants awaited. I slammed the door shut and pushed a large heavy chair into position before it.

I smiled at the maidservants, who were regarding the Geese with some dismay.

"I believe that I *could* do with a bath, thank you. If my lady-in-waiting, the Baroness of Breakabeen, wishes an audience, pray tell her that I am not to be disturbed." And I began removing my tattered dress.

'Twas a lovely bath, even though my doom, and the Prince's doom, were slowly, inexorably closing over our heads. The Geese enjoyed it too. They took turns joining me in the bath, which was perfectly enormous. We splashed one another and scrubbed and preened and finally hopped out again, all pink (me) and white (the Geese) and smelling like a gardenful of flowers (everyone in the room — we had managed to get the three maidservants rather damp too).

When we were out, we set about dressing in our wedding finery. I explained to the maidservants that the King wished the Geese to be present in their gowns and crowns. They cried out in wonderment over the little dresses and crowns, and then shyly approached the Geese to offer to assist them in dressing.

Much to my amazement, the Geese submitted to these attentions, standing quite still and behaving with perfect decorum while the young women slipped the dresses onto their bodies and placed the crowns neatly on their heads.

"Why, thou fickle flock of fowl! Thou wert never so mannerly for me!" I cried. But by then the women had turned to me and were holding the great golden gown up over my head, and my displeasure was smothered in heavy folds of cloth of gold.

When the dress was smoothed down over my form and my hair combed out (and the gold dust collected—the King had left very specific orders about that), the serving women sighed with pleasure.

"Look! Look how beautiful!" And they pulled a large looking glass out of the corner for me to see.

I made a face at the girl in the mirror. What was my beauty to me but a curse and a burden? Tho' I must concede that I looked positively ravishing. My hair, stupid thing, was evidently delighted to be going to a feast and had added some touches of its own. It had grown several feet, so that it reached the floor. Tiny roses and little yellow starlike flowers had appeared, woven through my locks and held by slender golden ribands.

My gown fitted me like a glove. The collar, stiff with embroidery, fanned out regally about my neck, while my bosom was partly exposed, the neckline swooping down prettily in a way which would perfectly show off the ruby necklace.

My attendants were grieved that my Geese should have crowns and I have none, but I assured them that the King was retaining my jewelry and would no doubt be using the ring for the wedding ceremony and the crown for my coronation as Queen. Satisfied, they let me go. They pulled the heavy chair away from the doorway, and I, treading as lightly as I might, warily peeked through the doorway.

Immediately, my arm was grasped by the Baroness and I was dragged into the outer chamber. I was beginning to be annoyed by this behavior, which seemed to be becoming a habit with Her Ladyship. I snatched my arm back, at some risk of tearing my sleeve.

"You wished to speak with me, madam?" I asked coldly.

The Baroness fixed me with a steely eye.

"Have you told him yet?"

"Have I told who what yet, Your Ladyship?" I asked.

"Have you told the King your name, you fool!"

The subject of my name also seemed to be becoming something of an obsession with the Baroness.

"No," I said, neglecting to add the customary title of honor.

"Then do not," she replied. "As you value your life, do not do so."

CHAPTER EIGHTEEN

Marriage Threatens

WEDDING IS DESTINY,
AND HANGING LIKEWISE.
— JOHN HEYWOOD, PROVERBS

I folded my golden arms under my golden bosom and tapped a glass-slippered toe.

"And why, pray tell, should I believe that my death would be disagreeable to you, my lady? In short, why should I trust you?"

The Baroness clenched her teeth and balled her fists, the very image of frustration.

"Because . . . because—O very well! I will do something for you if you promise not to tell him. Something you will like."

Hope, never long absent from my heart, began cautiously to rise again.

"What manner of thing might that be, Your Ladyship?"

"You love that bumbling blatteroon, the Prince of Dorloo, do you not?"

"No, certainly not," I said, offended. "'Twas only a tale I told to prevent you from guessing at his identity."

"That is not the tale your face told as you watched him being marched off this very afternoon."

"Your eyes are playing tricks on you, Baroness," I said firmly. "But get on with it. What favor had you in mind which involves the Prince of Dorloo?"

The Baroness fell silent for a moment. At last she said, "I will say no more than that I *think* that I can save his life." She closed her lips and folded her arms in turn. We faced one another, considering.

"You are in a position to set him free?" I asked.

"I believe so. I cannot be certain. There is ever an element of hazard in these affairs. If I do not succeed, you are free to say what you will."

I opened my mouth to accept, but then thoughts of self intruded and I bargained: "And myself also. You must let me go as well. Come, madam, you must see that if I am gone from here I cannot break my share of the contract. And I shall take great care never to meet up with the King again, I do assure you!"

But I spoke without any great confidence, for she started shaking her head almost as soon as I began to utter.

"No, no, no. I could not possibly free you both. I should be hanging a noose around my own neck. I am taking the utmost risk as it is."

"Very well," I sighed. "So be it."

Eagerly, she said, "You will need a name for the marriage certificate. What shall you say?"

"I care not," said I wearily. "You choose."

The Baroness cogitated. "Wilhelmina Frump," she suggested in the end.

"As you wish," I said. It made no odds to me; everyone would no doubt call me "Your Highness" in any case. I should not have the name "Wilhelmina Frump" ringing in my ears down all the days of my (brief) life.

"Let me give the signal then to my confederate below and he will go and do what he can to free the Prince." She went to the barred window and leaned out, making one forceful gesture, apparently to someone standing below. I followed her over and tried to see who 'twas, but whoever he might have been, he dodged out of sight too swiftly for me to see clearly.

"We must go down now," said the Baroness. "The King has sent for you twice already."

I bowed my head in acquiescence and we started for the outer door. She halted.

"O, I quite nearly forgot. I have something for you. It appears to be naught but a bit of trash, but the old hag was quite insistent, so if you wish it —" She rummaged about in the purse of her chatelaine as she spoke and at last held out a tiny packet, wrapped up with a bit of coarse sacking and twine.

"The old hag?" I queried, taking it from her. "Which old hag was that?"

"O, a queer old creature — she looked to be a hundred and twenty at the least, as shrunken and withered as a pumpkin in the springtime. Her nose and chin were so long they nearly met." The Baroness thought further, as a wild speculation was born in my brain. "O yes! She whistled as she spoke, because she possessed only two enormous teeth. Do you know her? Perhaps she is your mother," the Baroness suggested spitefully.

I replied that yes, I believed I did know who she was and that no, she was not my mother.

"She said that you were to drink the potion in that packet dissolved in a glass of wine just before your marriage ceremony. I imagine 'tis supposed to be some good luck potion. I do not know that I would obey, myself. That cloth looks rather grubby."

This was rather good coming from the Baroness, I thought, as the bosom of her dress was liberally spotted with grease stains and what appeared to be flecks of mustard and fried egg.

"Mayhap I should drink it now," I mused aloud.

"There is no time, and no wine to drink it with," she objected.

I nodded, concealed the little package in my left hand, and we left the room together.

There was a great crush of people gathered down below in the banqueting hall. Dinner had been put off, and a good number of people were therefore going hungry, awaiting the conclusion of my bath. An excellent way to be introduced to my new subjects.

Ah well. What did it matter? 'Twas the King's ill humor

that would rule my days, not that of anyone else in this room.

My Geese and I walked down the central staircase, not without some difficulty. The stair risers were not designed with Goose bodies in mind, and 'twas necessary for them to hop from step to step. This, combined with the fact that they were all decked out in their fine clothes, caused a smile to rise to the lips of many of those present.

We were led up to the King, where he sat at the head of the U-shaped table, toying with a large, ripe pear. As I watched, he held his little silver dagger between thumb and middle finger and playfully stabbed the fruit to the heart, several times.

He looked up as I approached and examined me from head to toe. He looked at the Geese, dressed in their regal garb, and snorted loudly. Then he shifted his regard back to me again. He nodded. "Quite an improvement, Goose Girl, though I will say that you looked better in river silt and rags than any maid I have ever seen before."

He turned to the assembled company and bared his pointed teeth in a dreadful smile.

"What think you all? Is she not every inch a Queen?"

"Indeed she is, sire!" trumpeted the entire party in one voice.

"And what think you of your new vassals, my dearest one?"

"You seem to have them well trained," I said coolly. "But then, you do hold the whip, do you not?" I had no particular desire to show the King a subservient face yet; I would wait for that until the whip descended upon my own back.

The crowd did not like my words. Many reddened; some with anger, but more, I think, with shame. The King, however, appeared to be delighted.

"A maid of spirit," he crowed joyfully. "What a prize have I captured!" He beckoned me forward. "Take this necklace on your wedding night, my sweet, as a gift from your husband-to-be." He held out the Ogresses' necklace. I took it and clasped it around my neck and then looked at my crown, which still lay on the table with the ruby ring. "These are to be yours hereafter, but not just at present," he said, closing his hand upon them. I shrugged and turned away.

The King now caught sight of the Baroness. "Come here, Lady Griselda, and rejoice with us. Have a glass of wine and drink a toast to our happiness. Everyone must drink a toast to our happiness. Steward!" I myself wondered if he had not already drunk a few toasts to our happiness while waiting for me. He seemed a bit exhilarated, though not intoxicated. He gestured to the steward, who set the servants circulating among the crowd with goblets of wine.

The King took three goblets from a silver salver and offered wine to the Baroness and myself.

"Here you are, Lady Griselda. Or Piggy, if I may be allowed to revive the dear old nickname." She took the wine, obviously just barely managing to restrain herself from biting the hand that proffered it. "And for my lovely bride —

what, by the by, is your name? The priest is bound to want to know."

The Baroness shot a commanding glance in my direction and obediently I responded, "Wilhelmina Frump, my lord."

"Wilhelmina Frump? Really? I would never have thought it. 'Tis of no moment, however. I shall never call you by it. Will you have some wine?"

"Since your majesty asks, I would rather have that pear, if you do not want it. I have had naught to eat today and am faint with hunger."

The King granted me rights to the mutilated pear with a stately wave of the hand. "Take this wine as well. 'Twill revive you. I don't want you swooning at the altar."

I snatched up the pear as quickly as was consistent with the behavior of a lady and greedily consumed it down to the last bite. A most important-looking cleric dressed in flowing robes approached the King and began discussing some detail of our wedding with him. Unobtrusively I moved a little apart from them. If I was to be bound body and soul to the King tonight I would savor what liberty I still possessed.

Had the Prince, I wondered, gotten aught to eat before being turned loose to make his way to freedom the best way that he might? I sighed. Most likely he had not. Still, with any luck, he *was* now free, while all I had was a pear and a glass of wine. There was no need to consider me unduly blessed.

As I thought this last thought, I heard the Prince's voice directly behind me. I froze like a rabbit under the hunter's gaze. What he had said I could not be certain, but the voice that spoke in answer was familiar to me as well.

"O no, no, sir! Come away at once," moaned Smeatt. Their voices, while near at hand, were oddly muffled. "'Tis most dreadful dangerous for ye here, I swear it! That lady means ye no good, but the most dreadful harm!"

"How dare you, Smeatt?" demanded the Prince loudly. I flinched, but no one else in the hubbub about us appeared to remark aught unusual.

"O, hush, sir, do!"

"That lady," continued the Prince, lowering his voice somewhat, "is the truest and bravest in all the world. Retract those words, Smeatt."

"Not *that* one! T'other one. That there Baroness. O, she's a subtle one, she is. Caught me afore I'd walked twenty paces ashore this mornin', an' sent me to steal ye out o' the dungeon an' kill ye in the woods, somewheres private, like. Why, I dunno, but she do be so subtle as a snake. An' o'course, seein' as how I've got that kind heart and ye have promised me that trunkful of gold—"

"I understand. Say no more." And happily, the two of them fell silent. After a few moments I turned casually around to see if I could observe them without myself being observed. Immediately I saw a large, lumpy bulge in the tapestry on the wall, from the bottom of which extended two pair of booted feet.

Little Echo also evidently had noticed this bulge, for she made for it with glad cries and, ducking her head under the tapestry, quickly wriggled her way back into the Prince's arms.

I removed myself from the vicinity of the bulge as rapidly as I might, having no desire to draw attention to this odd new feature of the wall hangings of the King's banqueting room. As I went, I considered the many things I should have to say to His Majesty the King of Dorloo if I ever got the chance. Imagine giving up a chance to escape like that! He and Smeatt and Little Echo were almost certain to be caught and executed on the spot.

The King chose this moment to break off his conversation with the distinguished cleric and, having ascertained to his satisfaction that his guests had the necessary fluids with which to drink to our eternal bliss, prepared to propose a toast. Strictly speaking, of course, he ought not to have done it — etiquette demands that another make the gesture — but the King was not the sort to care for that.

Forgetting for a moment his role as doting fiancé, he snapped his fingers at me and pointed at the floor next to his feet, thereby indicating that I had best move to my proper place by his side. I did so.

". . . And so I ask you, my loyal subjects, to drink to the long and fruitful reign of King Claudio the Cruel and Queen — What was your name again? O, never mind, it doesn't signify — Queen Whatsit here." Here he placed my crown upon my head and everyone bowed or curtsied, as the case might be.

I was paying little attention to this, but rather was occupied in watching the Baroness without appearing to do so. As she, I realized, was likewise watching me without appearing to do so.

When the company raised their glasses and drank, I did not raise mine. When the Baroness saw that, she lowered her own glass untasted.

"Why do you not drink to our happiness, Goose Girl, er, Queen?" enquired the King.

"'Tis not genteel for the subjects of a toast to drink to it," I said priggishly.

"Why, then," said the Baroness, "I will propose a toast to which you *can* drink with perfect propriety." She smirked evilly at me. "To the health of King Claudio the Cruel. May he live long!"

"I will drink to that!" said the King, and did so, but watched to see that I did so also.

I raised my glass and drank. The Baroness and all the guests followed suit.

The Baroness dropped her cup to the floor, half drained, and the contents splashed like blood on the stones. She raised one hand to her throat, one to her mouth. She staggered, and then sank to the floor.

"I am ill," she gasped.

At that moment, I felt a mighty tug on my gown. I looked down and saw that 'twas Ernestina, and in her mouth was the ruby ring which in the momentary confusion she must have stolen from the table before the King.

"O, Ernestina, not *now*," I whispered, for 'twas in my

mind to make our escape with those three behind the tapestry while everyone gathered about the Baroness.

Ernestina's eyes narrowed and she hissed. All the Geese save Little Echo gathered in a circle about me and advanced, hissing and clacking their bills in a threatening manner.

I hissed right back, "Stop! Stop it this moment! We must away!"

Alberta approached and grasped my left hand in her bill, the hand that had had the potion in it. That hand was empty now.

She pushed my hand toward the ring Ernestina held, but neither had the dexterity to slip the ring onto my third finger, where evidently they wished it to go.

"O, very well," I snapped, as we had already lost this heaven-sent opportunity. The Baroness, still gulping like a fish and clutching at her throat, was propped up on a serving woman's knee. People were beginning to look about themselves and call for a toad steeped in vinegar to revive the victim, or some leeches, or mayhap some goat droppings in wine.

I snatched the ring away from Ernestina and crammed it onto my finger, which it perfectly fit. I placed my hands on my hips and demanded angrily: "And what, pray tell, happens now, O my Geese?"

And never, ever, after that moment was my world the same.

CHAPTER NINETEEN

In Which
Fowl Is Now Fair

BEATEN WITH HIS OWN ROD.
— JOHN HEYWOOD, *PROVERBS*

There was a clap of sound, like wings, or thunder, then a blare of trumpets.

For some reason, I seemed to be *very* closely surrounded by a circle of young ladies of the King's court, all dressed alike, and all having the appearance of being much astonished and pleased about something.

I had no leisure to investigate this mystery at present, however. The noise had evidently startled the Prince and Smeatt from hiding. They stumbled out from behind the arras, blinking in the fading light.

The Prince, I saw, was now embracing an attractive young female dressed in ivory, who was clinging as tight to him as does a cockleburr to a lamb's wool.

I pushed aside the excitable young women. I sped to the side of the Prince and his female companion, took hold of her hair and pulled. She shrieked and fell back a pace.

"Unhand that Prince, thou hussy," I commanded sternly.

"But I do not want to, Alexandria," protested the hussy.

"Never mind what you want, young woman," I said. "What should concern you is what you will get if you do not immediately step away from that Prince." I took a firmer grip on her hair. She shrieked again.

Bang! The doors to the banqueting room swung wide. A horse and rider burst into our company, galloped through the crowd, and then came to an abrupt halt at our feet. The rider, who had been clinging precariously to the animal's back without benefit of saddle or bridle, immediately slid over its neck and landed in an undignified heap on the floor.

"Bucephalus!" cried the Prince in a joyful voice.

With an air of having successfully completed an unwelcome task, the horse shook itself all over. It then ambled over to the Prince and began to chew affectionately on his hair.

"O Bucephalus, I never thought to see thee in this world again!" said the Prince, embracing his equine friend.

The rider staggered to a standing position, muttering ominously and sending malevolent glances in the direction of the horse Bucephalus. She proved to be a diminutive crone with two tombstone teeth and a nose and a chin so long and curved that they nearly met in the middle. My Fairy Godmother, in fact. I regarded her with a certain lack of warmth.

"Shame on you, Alexandria Aurora Fortunato, to treat your ssissster sso!"

"I beg your pardon, madam?" I inquired politely, as is ever my way.

"And *look* at what you have done to this unfortunate Baronessss. Do you not know better than to ssslip unknown sssubsstances into other people's drinksss? Are you not ashamed of yoursself?"

"No, indeed, by my oath," I said, holding my chin up high. "She told me that potion was from you, but I did not believe her. She had no reason to wish me well."

The entire court, which had been transfixed by the recent events, looked from the hag to me; to the Prince, Smeatt, and the hussy; then to the circle of ladies in white; then to the Baroness and at last to the King.

At this he recovered the power of speech, of which he had seemed momentarily bereft. He let off an impressive string of curses, with which I will not sully your ears, and ended by demanding to know what the "old bag" thought she was doing bursting in upon his wedding like this.

Immediately the crone was all servile, bootlicking smiles.

"Why," she said, rubbing her hands together in a toadying sort of way, "I have come to bring you good luck, O graciousss King. Do you not know that charity to the poor is a blesssssing upon the rich? Essspecially on the occasion of your marriage, your Excellencssy." And she held out her skinny hand and whined, "Invite me to your wedding feasst,

198

O King, and you will live to see many days of plenty."

The King drew back his head and wrinkled his nose as though he smelled something unfresh, which mayhap he did. He crooked his index finger at the guard.

"Take this old witch out and give her a good ducking in the moat," he commanded. "If she be not dead at the end of it, you may let her go."

The hag nodded her head several times, appearing to be well satisfied with this reply. "Thank you, sire. 'Tis a great comfort to have my predictions so neatly vindicated. 'Twould have been mossst inconvenient had you after all bid me come to the feassst. The ssstory sssimply would not have turned out right, and I should have been put into the mossst frightful temper."

She lifted her hands up high and commenced tramping around in a circle, mumbling under her breath as she did so. The King appeared alarmed and the guard hesitated. When she had completed her third revolution she stamped her foot, flung her arms out in the King's direction, and shrieked in a quavering falsetto: "*T-z-z-z-zap!*"

The King was gone. Instead a gigantic, ungainly black bird with an ugly raw pink neck perched on the King's vacant chair. There was such a stench of death about it that all who stood near drew back in horror, clutching scented hankies to their noses. Several ladies swooned, but were restored to their senses by the mere entry into the room of a servant bearing the leeches, pickled toad, and goat-dung wine meant for the Baroness, so effective are these remedies on the afflicted.

The hag gave a self-satisfied chortle upon seeing the results of her incantations and said gleefully, looking about her, "That was good sssport, was it not? Well, what shall we do next?"

All those present immediately tried to arrange their facial muscles into expressions suggesting extreme compassion for the poor and did their best to remember the last time they had given a penny-piece to a beggar.

"Ah! That is right. The Baronessss!"

The hag skipped over to the recumbent Baroness, who appeared very ill indeed. The old lady bent over her, held out a withered hand, and whistled, "Ssspit it out!"

The Baroness did so. Once relieved of the potion, she improved dramatically. She sat up and no longer moaned but stared steadily into the eyes of the crone, who seemed displeased with her.

"Use my name to further your plotsss, will you? Well do I remember you, Madam Baronessss, from years ago! Piggy, they called you, because of your greedy ssspirit. Very well. Y'always wanted to marry that cruel-hearted ssso-called King over there"—she gestured at the giant Vulture perched on the King's carved chair — "and ssso you shall." She began her mumbling, foot-stomping dance once again.

The Baroness did not stir until after the final "*T-z-z-ap!*" when she stretched out her enormous black wings and flew to join the King on his chair. At first, he did not appear to wish to make way for her, but she screamed and pecked at him with her bloodstained beak and at length he shifted and gave her room to stand beside him.

"And now be off with you! Guard! Open that door!"

The guard, thoroughly intimidated by this time, hurried to do the hag's bidding. The great birds hoisted themselves up into the air and ponderously winged their way out of the Castle of Roseboom.

The hag nodded again, vigorously. "Time those two did a bit of good in their lives. Devouring decomposing corpssses may not ssseem like a good deed to mossst of usss, but it'sss all in Nature's Plan, all in the Cycle of Life. Why, I have longed to turn those two into Vultures for years."

"Then why did you not do so?" I demanded rather tartly. "It seems to me that we could have been spared a great deal of grief if you *had* done so some years back."

"Because, little Missstressss Sssuperior," hissed the old woman, turning back to me, "*you* had to go and fetch the crown jewels of Gilboa back before that could happen, did you not? I have a persssonal life too, you know. You can't expect me to do everything. My daughter-in-law is forever after me to mind the grandchildren, but have I a moment to call my own? I do not."

"The crown jewels of Gilboa?" I said blankly, my hand rising to rest on the glowing ruby necklace around my throat.

The hag cackled. "Yesssss! The very ones you are wearing

at this moment. You didn't know that that was what you were doing, did you? Never fret your little head, your ss-sissssters knew only too well. And now is the moment for your comeuppance, Missstressss Alexandria. Ernessstina Chrissstiana Fortunato, come forward and claim your inheritance!"

One of the young women in white (not the hussy, who had prudently withdrawn to several feet away from the Prince but was however sending a volley of languishing looks in his direction) came up to where we stood. She was a handsome young woman in the late twenties. She looked first at the hag and then at me. She smiled, hesitantly, and reached out a hand and touched mine.

"Hail, sister," she said.

"Give her the jewels," ordered the hag, baring her two tremendous teeth in a smile.

"The —?"

"The jewels! She's the rightful Queen of all Gilboa, ssso jusst you hand over the jewels!"

"I *beg* your pardon!"

"She's your sssissster, Dadgummit! The oldessst daughter of your mother and father! And the ressst of these females are likewise your ssisssters."

I scratched my head under the crown and considered this. "Have you some sort of legal proof?" I asked at length. "An entry in a parish registry, for example? Because I am the sole daughter of my parents that I know of, and I have never seen any of these women before in my life."

"O, but that is jussst what y'have done, Goossse Girl! Look around you. Where are your Geessse, pray tell?"

This in fact had been bothering me for some time. I had been made most uneasy with all these references to sisters, and I had several times looked around me for my Geese. Where indeed were they?

"I know not," I admitted. I further observed that there were twelve young ladies in white, provided you included the hussy, wearing white gowns and golden crowns with ivory and gold daisies on them, which were identical to, though much larger than, those belonging to my Geese.

To settle this matter, I turned to the Prince. "What, my lord, have you done with Little Echo?"

The Prince (or rather the King of Dorloo, for I kept forgetting to call him by his proper title) shook his head.

"I do not know, Mistress Alexandria. One moment I held Little Echo in my arms, a fine plump Goose. The next thing I knew, I found myself in intimate contact with that"— he pointed at the hussy, who simpered— "young woman. About this . . . lady's subsequent behavior I may say no more." And he folded his arms and sealed his lips chivalrously.

This seemed conclusive. For where else could Little Echo have gone? And by my vertu, I must confess that there was a look of Little Echo about the hussy's eyes, and in the way she held her head slightly cocked on her long neck.

She approached now, meeting my eyes. "If you do not believe that I am Little Echo, sister, then gaze upon this!"

And she pulled the fabric of her already sufficiently plunging neckline even lower, exposing a fresh scar on her left breast. "Here also you will see the wounds I have suffered in our search for our birthright," and she drew back the material of her left sleeve, showing another, though older, scar.

I nodded. "You are indeed Little Echo," I admitted. "And therefore I must believe that these other ladies are also my former fowl. But why must they be my sisters as well?"

CHAPTER TWENTY

Happily Ever After, More or Less

ALL IS WELL THAT ENDS WELL.
— JOHN HEYWOOD, PROVERBS

"*I* can tell you that, Alexandria," said the woman whom the hag had named Ernestina. "I am eldest, and remember it best. Indeed, I was of about your age when the Baron of Dwelly and Zeh rebelled against our father, the King of Gilboa, and most treacherously slew him as he dined in friendship at the castle of his Barony.

"The Baron of Dwelly and Zeh had long been promised to Griselda, the Baroness of Breakabeen, and they were allies in this, as in many other evil deeds. When our father lay weltering in his blood on the floor of the Castle of Zeh, the Baron instructed the Baroness to lure my mother with all of her twelve daughters to the Castle of Breakabeen under the pretext that our father had fallen gravely ill.

"When we arrived at the castle, we were immediately taken prisoner and handed over to a soldier for prompt execution. That soldier"— she shifted her gaze to the man standing next the Prince—"was Private Smeatt, at that time in the Baroness's employ. What she promised him in return for our deaths I cannot say, but as he is now in the royal army, I can only assume that some small degree of promotion was considered sufficient recompense for the deed."

Far from being embarrassed by this attention, Smeatt expanded like a rose in bloom. He removed his hat and bowed deeply to the company at large, smiling ingratiatingly all the while.

"Our mother bought our lives and safe conduct over the border from Smeatt," continued Ernestina, "with the crown jewels of Gilboa, jewels so precious to this land that it can never be happy, peaceful, or prosperous unless they adorn our Queen. How our dear Fairy Godmother obtained possession of the crown I cannot say—"

"He traded it for three bottles of rum and a sssackful of tobacco, two days after he got it, that's how," interrupted the hag. "'Twas not of a convenient shape to carry about, ssso he was pleased to see the back of it. I was pretending to be an old sssailor man at the time."

"—But we did hear that he fell into the hands of the Ogresses of Owlsville Valley, and had in turn to buy his own life with the necklace."

Ernestina paused for breath.

"But—pardon my mentioning it, but how did you become Geese? And how do I come into this story?" I asked.

Ernestina sighed. "I fear that we daughters were much to blame for that circumstance, at least as much as was our mother. As for you, Alexandria, why, our mother was with child when our father was killed, and that child was you.

"You see, when once Smeatt had seen us over the border into Dorloo, we were free—free to starve. We soon found the abandoned farmhouse which later became our home, so we were not without shelter. But our mother was a Queen and we were royal children. We did not know how to coax food from the soil and we were accustomed to luxury. Our mother, as I have said, was heavy with child and found work of any kind difficult.

"We children wept continually and quarreled amongst ourselves, crying for sweetcakes and wine. Our mother the Queen, made cross by her thirteenth confinement, finally called out in great vexation, 'Thou art naught but a lot of silly, quarrelsome Geese, my children!' And then, when yet one more daughter moaned and tugged on her garments, demanding sugar tarts to still the hunger pains, the Queen cried: 'O, how I do wish that thou *wert* a gaggle of geese, which might be satisfied with a sip of water and a sup of grass, for I do not see how I shall feed all of thee else.'"

Ernestina bowed her head. "I was but young, I know, yet I should have helped her more with the little ones. In a twinkling we twelve became white Geese. Our mother got her wish; born some months later, you were the only child left to her care. And Geese we have remained ever since."

I eyed the hag severely. "Had you aught to do with this?"

"Nay, I had not," she replied, much vexed. "I have had enough toil with your family without sssetting up more dif-

207

ficulties in my way. That horssse, for insstance." She glared at the horse. "'Tis true and I'll not deny that the beasst came and fetched me in the nick of time, but was it sstrictly necesssary to pound my bones to a jelly in the processss?"

No one replied to this query, so she resumed.

"One must be careful what one asksss for in this world, that is all. There are more ears lissstening than you think, essspecially on the edge of the wildwood. And sssome who lisssten have a queer sssense of humor. More than that I do not wish to ssay," and she closed her mouth with a snap.

I persisted. "But why was it necessary to find the crown jewels? Why could you not have changed the Geese back into Princesses?"

My Fairy Godmother turned purple with rage. "Do you think it is easy to alter sssomeone elssse's ssspell? The only way is to add a condition that is ssso difficult to meet that it will sssatisssfy the requirementsss of the ssspell. Ssso I sssaid that the daughters of the Housssse of Fortunato should remain domesssstic poultry all their days until and unlesss one of their blood wore the crown jewels of Gilboa again."

"I see," I said, thinking it out. "But —"

The old hag rolled her eyes.

I continued. "The Baroness, then, wished to prevent me from telling the King my name, because it was that of the real ruling house of Gilboa. So she pretended to free the Prince and arranged for my death, as she hoped, before witnesses. That way no one would know just how suitable a wife I was for King Claudio."

The hag nodded. "True enough. Had Claudio known who you were he would have watched over your health and safety like a broody mother hen. You would have given him the one thing he lacked: legitimacy. And long life was not in the plans that the Baroness had made for you."

"I suppose she would have suggested that I took my own life rather than marry the King," I brooded. "'Twas one way out, I will confess, but it had little appeal for me."

The crowd was growing weary of this lengthy analysis of events which did not directly affect them. They stared pointedly at their empty goblets and shuffled their feet.

Taking her cue, the hag said, "Now, are you sssatisfied that this is your eldessst sssissster Ernessstina? For if you are, you mussst yield up the jewels to her."

"O, very well," I said, and grudgingly unfastened the necklace, uncrowned my head, and slipped the ring from my finger. I did not mind the ring and the necklace, for I had never regarded them as mine, but 'twas *my* crown, and I loved it.

Ernestina handed me her gold and ivory coronet and donned the regalia I had put off.

"Behold the Queen of Gilboa," cried the hag. "Do you, people of Gilboa, accept Ernessstina Chrissstiana Fortunato as your lawful Queen?"

An elderly, stooped man came forward, and said, "Madam, I was once counselor to Good King Alfred of Gilboa, foully murdered by the Baron of Dwelly and Zeh. I recognize my King's features and those of his virtuous

Queen in the faces of these young women. I likewise recognize these as being the crown jewels of Gilboa. Hail, Queen Ernestina!"

"Hail, Queen Ernestina!" All the court took up the cry, and escorted Queen Ernestina to her throne room amongst a great tumult of jubilation. A few who had been close in the counsels of Claudio the Cruel slunk off and were never seen again, but the vast majority of those present were quite content to have a new mistress. They stamped their feet and shouted out, "Huzzah! Huzzah! Hooray!" until the very walls shook.

When all had departed rejoicing, I flung myself into a chair and inquired of nobody in particular, "Are we *never* to eat any dinner?"

"Mistress Alexandria — or rather, *Princess* Alexandria," said the King of Dorloo, appearing with a platter piled high. "Look! The cook came up from the kitchen to see what was the matter, and when I told her how hungry we were, she brought me this. See, she has given me these figs, and this cheese and dried meat. Will you not sit with me and eat?"

"You seem to have a way with cooks," I observed sourly, but sat down all the same.

"'Tis true enough," said the King peacefully. "They usually do seem to like me."

The horse Bucephalus accepted a fig from his master and began to chew. He then settled down to demolishing the rest of the fruit, this time without being asked.

"I have never thought of horses as *indoor* animals, exactly," I observed as the last fig disappeared down the creature's throat.

"Princess Alexandria, I must apologize," said the Prince. "I most deeply regret the hard words I spoke to you in the valley of the Ogresses, particularly with regard to my beloved horse Bucephalus, for now they do appear to be wholly unwarranted."

"You could not have known, my lord. Indeed, I took great care that you should *not* know, in order to mislead the Ogresses."

"'Twas neatly done, indeed. I never suspected. And so, do you then forgive me?"

"In certes I do," I said. "That is, I do if you will promise to forgive *me* for not telling you of the deception sooner and relieving your mind. I began to, once, but we were interrupted."

The horse, seeing that there was naught else fit to eat, began snuffling round my face with his large nose and drooling down my neck.

"Look!" cried the Prince in great delight. "He likes you!"

"Hmmm . . ." I said, concealing my enthusiasm with ease. However, I had some reason to be grateful to the horse Bucephalus and I am never rude, so I held my tongue.

The door opened and Little Echo reappeared from the throne room where, by the sound of it, a great deal of celebration was going on. Her eyes and feet were both dancing.

"Greetings, *little* sister of mine. You do understand that you are the youngest of thirteen now, do you not?"

"I do, sister," I said.

"And my name of course is not Little Echo—that is but a childish nickname. I am Elaine. I should prefer you to call me that from now on, little sister."

"I doubt that the occasion will often arise," I said, licking my fingers daintily.

Little Echo looked startled. "Why, how do you mean?"

"I mean that if the King of Dorloo will permit, I was born his subject and I mean to return to the home our mother left us in the land of Dorloo, there to pursue the perfectly happy life I led until our mutual Fairy Godmother began interfering in my life."

"O, but you cannot!" she cried.

"No?" I inquired, lifting one eyebrow. "And why is that?"

"Because this is your real home now, here with us."

"I would like to see you stop me, *Little Echo*," I said.

"O, dear," she said, wringing her hands. "I only meant to tease you a trifle, to pay you back for your imperious ways over the years. If the others thought I had put you against us I should be in such trouble—"

"Here you are, my sisters, Your Highness." 'Twas one of my other siblings. By the size of her lower extremities I deduced that 'twas Cassandra Big Foot. I supposed I would be wise to address her solely as Cassandra from now on. "We wondered where you were. Alexandria and King Edmund are quite the heroes of the night and we wish to toast your health. That is"—she inclined her head courteously toward us—"if you are not too fatigued with your adventures."

Little Echo leaned forward and whispered furiously in my ear. "You see? They want you. We want you dreadfully. You were our lone hope in all of those years, especially after Mother died. I pray you do not desert us now, for I know I shall die if you do. I'll not have time to die of heartbreak, however, for Ernestina will draw and quarter me first."

I meditated upon this.

The King of Dorloo broke in. "As much as I should like to have you as my subject again," he said, taking my hand in his and speaking gravely, "I believe that your place is here, with your family. You would be most dreadfully lonely, you know, without your beloved Geese."

I thought of our little cottage in the wood. I imagined my life there, quite solitary. Perchance a cow might provide some companionship; I could surely afford one now. King Edmund, no doubt, would come to visit me now and again, but yet — 'Twas true 'twould not be at all the same.

Slowly I nodded my head.

"I could try it here, I suppose, just for a time," I said.

"Hurrah!" shouted Little Echo (or Elaine). "Come into the throne room and we will tell the others!"

And she pulled me to my feet (incidentally disengaging my hand from the King's) and dragged me forcibly along.

As we went, she murmured for my ear alone, "Did you speak true to the Baroness? You said that you do not love Edmund. Because if you do not, may I have him? I think he is just *wonderful*. You cannot imagine how kind and good he was to me in the dungeons of Castle Breakabeen."

"My dear sister Elaine," I said, through clenched teeth. "I believe I have already told you to keep your distance from the gentleman in question."

"O, so then you *do*—!"

I placed my palm firmly across my new sister's mouth. Whether in human or Goose shape, she was clearly going to be a pest and a botheration to me.

I half turned to look at King Edmund following in our train. Mayhap, I mused, I would have to finish that last stitch on my wedding gown one of these days, after all.

Someone needed to keep an eye on the King of Dorloo.

And that someone most assuredly was not going to be Little Echo.

The End